ALLAN MORRISON is a prolific auth
books include *Goanae No Dae That; Last Tram Tae
Auchenshuggle; Haud ma Chips Ah've Drapped the Wean;*
and *Should've Gone Tae Specsavers, Ref!;* His media
appearances include *The One Show, Richard and Judy,*
STV's *Riverside Show, The Fred McAulay Show* and BBC
Radio's *Out of Doors.*

Allan is involved in charity work, is a speaker at various
events, enjoys hill-walking, sport and travel. He and
his wife live in the West of Scotland and he is the proud
grandfather of four grandchildren. Allan is an ardent
'undecided' voter, and as such is unsure whether Big Nellie
Nellis would have got his vote.

'Naw First Minister!'

Irascible Big Nellie Nellis Becomes Scotland's
First Minister... pity help Scotland!

ALLAN MORRISON

with illustrations by
BOB DEWAR

Luath Press Limited
EDINBURGH
www.luath.co.uk

First Published 2015

ISBN: 978-1-910745-17-5

The author's right to be identified as author of this work under
the Copyright, Designs and Patents Act 1988 has been asserted.

The paper used in this book is recyclable. It is made
from low chlorine pulps produced in a low energy,
low emissions manner from renewable forests.

Printed and bound by
CPI Antony Rowe, Chippenham

Typeset in Sabon and MetaPlus by 3btype.com

Contents

NOTE: All Scottish Parliament characters in this book are
entirely fictitious and in no way relate to anyone living or dead.

Acknowledgements

My sincere thanks go to Mark Philip Jones, Craig Morrison, Lynne Roper, Archie Wilson, John and Morag Wilson, plus various other voters who must collectively share the blame for *Naw First Minister!*

Preface

SCOTLAND'S PARLIAMENT is no longer in its infancy, having been in existence since the 1 July 1999 when it was first convened in a temporary location at the Mound, Edinburgh. Subsequently it moved to its permanent home at the Scottish Parliament Building at Holyrood, with the first debates taking place on 7 September 2004.

During this time it has matured into an established seat of government, taking on the many characteristics of parliaments and governing bodies worldwide. Politicians in Scotland are now just like their counterparts elsewhere, making it high time to poke some fun at our homegrown political machine.

Scottish Parliament characters in *Naw First Minister*

FIRST MINISTER
Nellie Nellis (Referred to as 'Big Nellie', plus a multitude of very naughty words used by her political enemies).

DEPUTY FIRST MINISTER
Murdo McAlpine (Referred to as 'Alaska', always seeking advice from Nellie. Is seen by many as a bit of a Uriah Heep).

BIG NELLIE'S TRUSTY PA
Fraser MacLeod (Known as 'Razzle Dazzle' because of his blonde locks). Responsible for speechwriting, political research and strategy.

SCOTTISH LABOUR LEADER
Brian Duddy (Known as the 'Dud').

SCOTTISH CONSERVATIVE AND UNIONIST PARTY LEADER
Alex Humphrey (Known as 'Humph'... as in 'Gets up everybody's humph').

SCOTTISH NATIONAL PARTY LEADER
Neil Forbes (Known as 'Domestos', as he is
considered by many to be round the bend).

SCOTTISH GREEN PARTY LEADER
Diana Duncan (Referred to as 'Neon',
a right tube if ever there was one).

SCOTTISH LIBERAL DEMOCRAT LEADER
Tom Smith (Known as 'Thrombosis',
considered a bit of a clot). Someone who has
fallen down the political ladder.

PRESIDING OFFICER
Jeanie Cameron (Known as 'Genie', shouts
'Order, order', and seems to magically appear
when someone opens a bottle).

**CONVENER OF ECONOMY, ENERGY AND
TOURISM COMMITTEE**
James Nevis (Called 'Ben').

CONVENOR OF FINANCE COMMITTEE
George Woods (Known as 'Wonga').

**CONVENOR OF RURAL AFFAIRS, CLIMATE
CHANGE AND ENVIRONMENTAL COMMITTEE**
Hugh Rae (Known as 'Hip Hip').

'See that Scottish Parliament Building, it looks like a bingo hall frae the front, a Hong Kong brothel at the back, and it's got mair deadwood than the stockade at the OK Corral. Furthermore, it produces mair gas than the hale o' the North Sea.'

BIG NELLIE NELLIS

Introduction

*N*AW FIRST MINISTER! takes a radically different
political path to that of the wonderful BBC series,
Yes Minister.

Yes Minister featured the ongoing battle of wits
between civil servants and their political masters. *Naw
First Minister* stars Big Nellie Nellis as First Minister,
who, fed up with politicians' machinations, makes it her
ambition to 'sort that lot oot' at Holyrood, a place
where she says people eat and drink too much and do
nothing but pick
cleverly worded
fights in a labyrinth
of deceit.

Whether at St
Andrew's House,
which accommodates
part of the Scottish
Government, or at Bute
House, the First Minister's
official residence, or at the
Parliament Building, this
self-assured mistress of
plain speech doesn't
miss and hit the
wall when it
comes to laying

BIG NELLIE NELLIS
FIRST MINISTER

out her ambitions. She's not slow to express her contempt for a prescriptive parliament with its apparently piffling rules. Even MSPs infamously renowned as 'no wallflowers' are routinely brushed aside by a nicotine-spewn bark of contemptuous, unparliamentarily caustic language several decibels louder than the average person's, a trait which serves to increase Big Nellie's formidable status. Pompous, pretentious, flippery, stodgy old-stagers, blowhards and any turbo-charged hecklers are quickly punctured. Individuals having fruity twangs to their voices are particular targets, and now look at Nellie open-mouthed with the fixation of the mildly deranged.

Many established members are thrown aside with this seismic shift, or indeed tossed to the baying mob despite the prompting of party spin-doctors. A number of MSPs who have clearly failed in their attempts to unsettle Big Nellie through tantrums, bust-ups, battles of wits, stooshies and power plays, have caused much media gossip leading to them being deselected by mutinous local associations, given the heave-ho, and whizzed into oblivion.

Opponents have found her cerebral chutzpah and tidal wave of directness of speech unusual in the political field. They find her verve deceptive, especially with her scathing attacks when the diaphanous mists of anger seem to wreathe around her head and she sweeps through opponents like a wrecking ball. Anyone launching a stealth campaign against her, or trying to be king-of-the-castle, is in for a rude awakening for Nellie always seems to win full-blown stairheid rammies.

What the spellbound listeners, hanging onto her every word, assume to be off-the-cuff remarks are, in a small number of cases, the result of Nellie's tooled-up preparation, designed to give a memorable sound bite. This can sometimes be creative in the primal Caledonian unpleasantness-inflicting department, hitting below the belt. Her true overall genius can however be heard in some absolute belter of a bolt-from-the-blue inspired phrase, delivered with stone cold unshakeable certainty. She's certainly a self-assured extrovert with a razor-sharp mind, an unquenchable optimist, and with a talent for pricking pomposity while very, very occasionally delivering a line in self-deprecation. This lady enjoys being a serial winner and is a law unto herself.

When the harassed Presiding Officer in the debating chamber shouts, 'Orrrder!', the command is immediately ignored by the First Minister with Big Nellie steadfastly continuing to hammer home her points, her voice only changing in volume and speed.

Politicians are normally selective about appearing on television and radio programmes where they can be interrogated by interviewers keen to make their mark on unsuspecting victims. In Nellie's case broadcasters are now most reluctant to lock verbal horns, fearing her robust style of communication and general demeanour. She has proved impervious to all their interrogation techniques. Nellie's steely gaze, forever backed up by a unique intellect and wisdom achieved from life's school of hard knocks, would certainly frighten most. There were scuttlebutt rumours that some of her family were into organised crime in Glasgow; therefore it was only logical Nellie chose the disorganised criminal scene of the Scottish Parliament.

But no one should envy the scale of the challenge facing Nellie in this most testing of jobs, especially sorting out the hellish merry-go-round of committee meetings much favoured by MSPs, dodging responsibility while scratching around for controversies with which to feed their party leaders' egos. However, as Nellie thinks in the most simplistic of terms, and is usually able to quickly analyse any situation, it is not so easy for her opponents.

The basic problem for the other parties, now riven by backbench in-fighting, is that there is scant prospect of removing her with a vote of no confidence as her poll ratings in Scotland have risen to astronomical heights, and she has enough feral instinct to scent the breeze and kill off any aspiring challenge.

It was necessary for Nellie, as First Minister, to have a deputy. Having seen the new First Minister in action, the party leaders insisted that an established, well-respected MSP be appointed. He lasted almost three months before his ever increasing blood pressure triggered a heart attack. Next up for this key role was a recognised *apparatchik* of the Scottish political scene, someone who had been in politics all of his adult life. He made it past three months before her hair-trigger temper caused a nervous breakdown. Finally, Murdo McAlpine, a soft-spoken Highlander was persuaded to take on the post. Certainly it was no dream ticket. However, McAlpine sensibly opted for a low profile, apparently deciding just to go along with Nellie's proposals and opinions.

Big Nellie's leadership and roguish glamour has attracted enormous popular and critical acclaim well beyond Scotland. Many of her manifesto proposals have been seen not just as innovative, but visionary. Indeed, her international appeal now commands respect and deference. She has been voted Scotland's top celebrity, the best export since macaroon bars and, with her image and quotes continually appearing on news and social media throughout the globe, tourism has significantly increased.

The philosopher, Isaiah Berlin, once said that the art of great leadership should be founded on personal instinct, flair and judgement. Big Nellie's got them in spades!

'At the annual Scottish Parliament ceilidh ah saw aw they MSPs dancin' the Barn Dance... sidestep, sidestep; back sidestep, sidestep; wan step back, wan step forward, then go roon an' roon... typical!'

BIG NELLIE NELLIS

CHAPTER ONE

In the beginning was the word

... and for Big Nellie Nellis the word was 'cockup'.

IT WAS ON a dreich night in February when she bought a fish supper on her way home from her job as senior supervisor in a clothing factory in Glasgow. The fish supper was, as usual, tasty. Tony always sold excellent fish, encased in rich, mouth-watering batter. But as Nellie devoured her meal at her Maryhill flat, she also read the contents of the old newspaper in which the delicious food was wrapped. It was *The Guardian*, not a paper she would normally take, and it was an article on the Scottish Parliament Building in Edinburgh that caught her eye:

> The Fraser Report, an inquiry into the way in which the £431 million building was procured, is due to be published. Having listened to 43 days of evidence and shifted his way through some million or more words, Lord Fraser is likely to declare, although in more measured terms than this, that the greatest building project in recent Scottish history has been a cockup, and on an epic scale.

Nellie exploded.

'Four hunner and thirty wan million pounds! It certainly is a cockup. And ah can't even get Glasgow Council tae fix ma windae. They wid be better in a village hall, fur they MSPs are aw eejits. Politicians jist gae me the boke. Useless! Ah could do a better job wi ma arms tied behind ma back. Disnae matter which party you vote for, aw you get are politicians. If ah wis in that Scottish Parliament, ah wid fair go ma dinger.'

Nellie tidied away the remnants of her supper, opened the windows to get rid of the smell, and gave her flat a spot of dusting, and it was at that moment in time Big Nellie Nellis decided on her new career. To save Scotland from its politicians, and to stop them wasting *her* smackaroonies!

So, a determined Nellie duly went about the business of getting herself elected to the Scottish Government, eventually standing on a most interesting, if not to say ambitious, manifesto. And the voters in her constituency just loved her poster slogan and mantra: 'Big Nellie: the very man tae sort them oot!'

Crowds flocked to her campaign meetings to hear her unique brand of rhetoric.

'Ladies and gentlemen, chronically weak administrations in the Parliament have consigned generations tae wither away in auld schools, tae live their days trapped within the borders of huge, violent, grim housing estates with rubbish-strewn strips of dark streets, and used syringes glistening in the light from a few broken lampposts. Then us folks die years afore we should. Oor Scottish psyche leads us to expect life to be disappointing and unsatisfactory. Life should no' be endured, but be pleasurable. We should all have fun!

'We should spend Scotland's money on essentials, not on funny auld constructions like that Parliament Building or ideological follies. We require a 21st century enlightenment for this country's people. That's why ah'm here, tae fix everythin' fur ye!'

The press just loved it. That and Big Nellie's election manifesto:

- £500 pounds winter fuel allowance for everyone over 65.

- Subsidised holidays in Scotland for all Council Tax payers.

- Free transport on ferries, buses and trains for everyone over 60 who is not working.

- All wheelie bins to be collected weekly.

- Pot holes filled in within 24 hours.

- Sir Andy Murray to be appointed Sports Minister.

- The tax on whisky to be cut by ten per cent and all adults to receive a bottle of Glenmorangie at Hogmanay.

- Free haggis to be supplied for Burns Night.

- Scotland's National Anthem to be changed to 'I'm Gonna Be (Five Hundred Miles)' by the Proclaimers.

- Improve the calibre of MSPs by insisting that all candidates should hold at least a Scottish National Qualifications Certificate in drawing.

- All MSPs must actually have worked prior to standing for Parliament.

- All MSPs must do something useful for once. They must devote one day each week to the ongoing maintenance and cleaning of the Parliament Building in order to save the annual two million pounds maintenance costs.

- Voting should represent the wide breadth of ages in Scotland: sixteen-year-olds should get a vote; experience should be recognised by giving two votes from 40 years of age; wisdom, experience and age should be recognised by giving three votes to those of 60 and over.

- Voting should be compulsory.

- Fracking should take place under the Scottish Parliament Building to capture the vast amount of gas accumulated from the corridors of power above.

The high profile campaign which followed caused considerable consternation among her fellow candidates. Nellie's sometimes plain-spoken, sparky and outrageous statements were derided by the media but loved by the Scottish public at large.

And come the election it proved to be an absolute skoosh for Big Nellie.

When she arrived at the Scottish Parliament Nellie found that no political party had achieved a majority in this boiler room of power. All the major parties bickered as to who should get the top job of First Minister, and finally an ostrich-like decision was made. It was decided it should go to this new, neutral, MSP, Nellie Nellis, of the AGSTLO (Ah'm Gonnae Sort This Lot Oot) party, someone below the radar, and a newcomer they all thought could be manipulated. What a mistake! They should have listened to the Holyrood chatterati and cherry-picked a safe pair of hands. Now they were left tying themselves in knots over their hasty appointment. It was political speed dating at its worst with Nellie now at the centre of the political spectrum.

❖ ❖ ❖

The dull May day with its seamless grey clouds pressed down on Edinburgh.

The assembled press corps filed into the First Minister's official residence of Bute House at 6 Charlotte Square, zoom lenses and hand-held woolly-grey covered mikes at the ready. They were there to listen to Scotland's new leader, and hopefully to eat freshly cut sandwiches washed down with copious amounts of beer, wine, and perhaps some of her single malt.

They dutifully shuffled through the narrow entrance

into a small lobby, and turning right, made their way, single file, up the winding staircase to the drawing room with its continental glass chandelier and full-length portrait of the 3rd Earl of Bute, the first Scottish-born British Prime Minister.

With its limited space the drawing room only just managed to accommodate the invited hacks.

Bute House, looking directly onto Charlotte Square, was at one time owned by the 4th Marquess of Bute, but in 1966 was conveyed to the National Trust for Scotland. It then became the grace-and-favour residence of the Secretary of State for Scotland who remained there until Scottish devolution in 1999. It is here that the weekly meeting of the Scottish Government's Cabinet is held, together with ministerial receptions and press conferences.

At the scheduled time of 11.00am the First Minister appeared from her living accommodation, caught in the silvery strobe of camera flashes, every eye following her movement. A rotund, buxom woman of perpetual middle-age and formidable appearance with a big baw-face that appeared freshly scrubbed, accentuated with bright red lipstick generously applied to seemingly ever moving lips. The First Minister was high-rumped, with long legs which looked as though they could stretch into different time zones, and bosoms requiring their own postcodes, while an occasional bark betrayed her inability to give up a 20-a-day habit.

The press throng duly noted Nellie's wardrobe of a

red and black business suit, accompanied by candy pink nail varnish, a chunky charm bracelet on her right wrist, and leopard-print peep-toe shoes. The sleekness of her mahogany bob made Anna Wintour look like a prize poodle. The sweet, opulent smell of perfume, like the cosmetics counter in Fraser's, filled the air. This was a woman who knew who she was, and liked it.

As Nellie made her way to the podium, the outside world suddenly became distant, and, as the eager flow of chatter ceased, an expectant air filled the room.

Donning her heavy, dark-rimmed glasses her gravitas upped a gear, and her seemingly x-ray eyes pierced the admiring souls of the assembled press-pack.

'Good morning, guys,' Nellie began, as she beamed in the warm glow of flashbulbs, enjoying the sort of high-pressure occasion that her metabolism was obviously built for. 'Ah'll give ye a wee spiel first then ah'll take questions. Ah'm no' saying ah'll answer them,' she laughed. Depends if ah like them.

'This is like the changing o' the guard. Ah'm the new drill sergeant in charge of the troops. So, first of all let me tell you this Parliament requires a fix. There's gonnae be a stramash an' plenty o' argy-bargy. This is the dawn of a new political era. How dae ah know? It's because the voters have spoken.

'The usual suspects have put forward dull temptings full o' sterile dross. Most have their thumbs in their bums and their minds in neutral. Let me tell you something. All the parties' policies may appear to be different at first glance but they have wan shared characteristic: they are not based on realism but merely the whim o' some wee self-important fella pulling the strings in the background.

'It is clear that politics attracts more than its share o' emotionally unintelligent philistines with their cockamamie cack-handedness. All of the parties have their own dogma, but they are like skaters oan thin ice at the Lake of Mentieth; ready to go under at any moment when the cracks in their arguments appear. What we have is a political machine operated by unappealing inadequates.

'The voters are mostly ill-informed, normally by youse lot, and are the reason the other parties feel safe. They may have been promised the earth, but MSPs know deep doon they will never be able tae deliver whit they have spouted.

'It is clear that this country requires genuine change. So forget the usual smoking mirrors. Ma party, the "Ah'm Gonnae Sort This Lot Oot' party", with its uniquely excellent policies will ensure that the production values o' this tedious soap opera wull be radically improved. So the public need to support ma party rather than the other "do-sod-all" parties.

'For instance ah have already found that Holyrood's committees are the windiest, dullest, snoriest, most self-regarding, hubristic and snooziest ah have ever encountered. They have all obviously had a humour bypass. More air is expended than effort. Instead they should be working hard for Scotland's people. Ah have had a better time at my dentist, although after ten minutes sitting in their committee meetings ah feel well an' truly anaesthetised an' ready fur an extraction.

'Politics requires tae be saved from the same auld perpetual nappy-wearing politicians continually doing the square root o' bugger all. People have choice and empowerment in most areas o' their lives, and they don't know it. They will not continue forever tae vote for talking heads with their flawed rhetoric that cannot spend our finances wisely. Scotland was revitalised by the Industrial Revolution. Now it's gonnae be revitalised by the Nellie Revolution.

'And you lot, the media, do nothing but display contempt for the intelligence o' the electorate. You make a right hoo-hah over nothing for your own petty ends, just to try and increase your circulation. So listen, guys, let's all pull thegither for the good o' oor wee country.

'Ah'm here tae stop wasting Scotland's money, tae destroy cartels, an' tae upset the cosy traditional order in this Parliament. So, just watch this space.

'Noo, ah'll take questions, guys. Good wans noo, or ah'll gie ye a red card!' Nellie smiled wickedly.

The first brave soul, a sandy haired young fellow, got to his feet. 'William Jones frae *The Scotsman*. That was quite a speech, First Minister. A bit of a stonker if I may say so. Even I am impressed. Do you really think, First Minister, that our electoral system in Scotland is truly democratic?'

'Well, Wullie, first of all ah'm fair glad that you are impressed. Let me tell you that not all of the electorate will vote at the next election. But ah can gie ye a guarantee that 100 per cent o' the electorate will moan aboot the result regardless of whit it is. That, my friend, is true democracy.'

'But sometimes, First Minister, don't you feel that, with our Single Transferable Vote system whereby each person can be represented by one of eight MSPs, is over the top from a democratic point of view?'

'Not at all,' replied Nellie. 'Wan of them can be the designated driver.'

'Perhaps I could just ask one more question, First Minister,' asked the young reporter, clearly wanting to make the most of his opportunity. 'Could I have your views on how long a MSP should serve?'

'That's up tae the judge, Son. Next!'

'First Minister, Adam Pilchard from *The Herald*.' An older bearded individual with thick glasses had stood up. 'You have already acquired a reputation for speaking your mind. In fact you have just demonstrated that with our friend from *The Scotsman*. Don't you have a wee voice in your head that stops you saying things that are, shall we say, outspoken and not always politically correct? Perhaps you could also be slightly more diplomatic and tactful.'

'Believe me, Adam, ah was never outspoken by anyone. And just so you know ah don't tell porkies, only expedient exaggerations. And let me tell you further that people who are diplomatic are usually jist folks who say, "nice doggy, nice doggy," until they can lay their hauns oan a half brick. Anyway tact is just for people who aren't witty enough tae be sarcastic. Next.'

Adam sat down slowly with a perplexed look on his face. A tall, rough looking man with a leery smile arose. He had a crooked posture and a distinctive scar ran across his mouth and chin.

'First Minister, Henry Spiro, freelance journalist. We seem to know very little about you. You have come into politics with apparently a non-political background. You are a political nobody. Do you really believe you have the proper skills for the job?'

Nellie took an immediate dislike to this man and his impertinent question. His attitude was cold and calculating.

'If ah'm a political nobody, Henry, then let me tell you *nobody* is perfect. So that means ah'm perfect. And ma political skills are jist fine. Let me tell you also that it seems to me that politics in Scotland is the art of looking fur trouble, finding it everywhere, diagnosing it incorrectly, an' then applying unsuitable remedies. An' ah'm jist the wee wummin tae fix it. Apart frae findin' Shergar ah can do most things. As for ma family background, ah have one son who lives with me at present here in Bute House.'

'If I may ask you a follow-up question, First Minister,' continued Spiro. 'As you are now living in Edinburgh, as a Glaswegian, what do you think of Edinburgh?'

'Certainly you may ask, Henry. Ah think Edinburgh is great. And another good thing aboot it is that it's only a short flight away frae Scotland. Next.'

This caused quite a bit of laughter round the room.

A tall, tweedy individual of around 50 stood up. Nellie couldn't quite make up her mind if it was a toupee or a somewhat amateur dye job, all supported by fashionable chin stubble.

'First Minister, Peter Kinnoch from *The Aberdeen Press and Journal*. You're making quite an impact on the Holyrood scene and you haven't been here long. What is there about you that has got people talking?'

'Thanks for saying ah'm making an impact, Peter. But listen. You don't applaud the singer fur clearing her throat. Ah haven't even started tae sing properly yet.'

'I said, First Minister, that you have people talking. But were you aware that according to a recent study 89 per cent of the Scottish population don't know who their MSP is?'

'Ah'm amazed, Peter! Imagine 11 per cent actually know who their MSP is. Listen, ah have listened tae long winded, shallow, waffling, tedious pronouncements fur too long. The public, oor constituents, demand more; not a group of individuals who are only capable o' constitutional navel gazing or joining the wind section of an orchestra. In other words, doing nothing but blowing their own trumpet. Politics can obviously do terrible things. It can bend people oot o' shape; make them say things that are palpably untrue; coarsen, tarnish an' trash guid folks. Next.'

A large lady wearing a shapeless blue blouse, so long in the sleeves that only her chewed fingernails were visible, got to her feet.

'First Minister, Sarah Rankin from the *Record*. If I may be quite frank, it has already been alluded to that you are not averse to dealing in underhand tactics and are utterly ruthless. Is this true? Also, don't you think you're punching above your own weight?'

'If ah may take one question at a time. Of course ah can be ruthless, Sarah. Ah'm a heat-seeking missile lookin' for trouble. Ah'll do anything tae improve the lot o' the Scottish people. Efter aw, ah'm noo a politician. And am ah punching above ma weight? Ah hope so. Like every ither women, including ah see yerself, ah try to keep ma weight down.'

'Oh! A bit personal, First Minister, but never mind. Just one more question. What do you think of a free market economy?'

'Ah think it's unfair. These stallholders are there to make a couple o' bob. Jist kiddin' ye, pal,' she laughed. 'But let me be serious for a minute. Mainstream politics have tae be rehabilitated. This seamless illusion of efficiency cannot go on. Money has tae be spent wisely. The Scottish Government is forever wasting everybody's hard earned smackeroonies. We cannot be forever paying oor bills on the "never-never".

An' if you don't like ma proposals, and some o' you have already criticised them, ah have plenty mair. Remember whit the immortal Groucho Marx said, "These are my principles, and if you don't like them... well, I have others!"'

Sarah Rankin continued. 'First Minister, what about that other market, the Common Market?'

'Well, personally ah've got to say, Sarah, that ah've picked up quite a few bargains at the Barras in Glasgow. Next!'

A reporter slouching on his chair with a laid-back, cavalier appearance spoke up. 'First Minister, Joseph Purdue from the *Edinburgh Evening News*. We know little of your background apart from you having a son. Are there any other politicians in your family?'

'Sure, Joseph. Ma cat is a Tory, an' ah'll tell you how ah know. He's a tom, and goes around Charlotte Square every night screwing aw the other cats. Next.'

'First Minister, Emily Brown from BBC Scotland *Newsnight*. How optimistic are you about Scotland's economic future? In other words, are you an optimist or a pessimist? So, First Minister, is your glass half full or half empty?'

'Listen, Emily. It depends whit's in ma glass.'

'May I follow up with a personal question, First Minister. There seems to be some confusion regarding your age. May I ask how old you are?'

'Sure, Emily. Ah'm 55.'

'But hold on, First Minister, that's apparently the age you quoted some years ago.'

With apparent difficulty, Nellie held her displeasure in check. 'Aye, Emily, ye see ah'm no' like other politicians. Ah like tae stand by what ah say. Anyway you know whit is said, time waits for no man, but it always stands still for women. Next.'

'First Minister, James Wilson from CNN.' The accent was unmistakably New York. 'There has been much consternation about some of the proposals in your manifesto. Particularly the one where you would expect MSPs to be responsible for the maintenance and cleaning of the Parliament Building. Surely these individuals didn't come into politics to do such work?'

'Jimmy, I have produced what you Americans might describe as a veritable smorgasbord o' tasty opportunities fur ma manifesto. Furthermore, let me tell you that MSPs should be an example tae their constituents and demonstrate their commitment tae working, and also to minimise all costs associated with Parliament. This will show the Scottish electorate those MSPs who are dedicated tae this country and those who are not.'

'But surely, First Minister, it's not as if getting your manifesto through is a slam dunk. You are not really in a strong position to implement all these new ideas. What you will need is a working majority in cahoots with some of the mainstream parties.'

'Listen, ma friend. What Scotland needs is the

majority working... and that is what ah intend to achieve.'

'But, First Minister, when a great many people are unable to find work, unemployment results,' continued the American.

'Brilliant! An absolutely brilliant conclusion!'

'Just one further question, First Minister. What is your position regarding the Middle East.'

'That's easy. Ah want tae see Falkirk flourish. Next.'

A slightly brittle-looking lady, somewhat glam in designer sunglasses, got to her feet.

'First Minister, Mairi McNaughton from *The Dundee Courier*. Would you agree that Scotland is a land of great promise?'

'Aye, Mairi. Especially in election years. It's called political doublespeak, a sort of arms race of rhetoric between the parties. And also let me tell you, in politics talk is cheap and that's because supply exceeds demand.'

'But, First Minister, all of the parties — and there is quite a selection to choose from — make various promises to all and sundry. However, most voters still seem to be settled on one party or another. Do you think there really are many swing voters?'

'Listen, Mairi, I don't care whit the punters' sexual preferences are,' she laughed, 'as long as they vote for me.'

The *Courier* reporter sat down with a pained look on her face.

A youngish man wearing tight cream slacks and a pair of tasselled loafers was next up.

'First Minister, John Sidebottom from *Associated Press*. As has been already stated, you have really come out of nowhere into the political arena. Following the latest election a number of other new MSPs have also arrived at Holyrood. Some of them are reputed to be bright sparks. It is well known that the established parties wanted a First Minister who was neutral and acceptable to them. Why do you think you were selected as First Minister rather than perhaps any of the other new MSPs?'

'Good question, John,' said Nellie as she emitted one of what would become her trademark full-throated laughs. 'You could say that ah wis just unlucky or you could say the country is lucky tae have me. Perhaps it was for ma diplomacy skills, eh? Time will tell. As for the new bright sparks coming on board that is great as they can help me fire up the rest o' the MSPs, for the old ones are like a coo sittin' oan top of a flagpole at the Parliament Building: everyone knows it didn't get there by itself; it certainly doesn't belong there; it doesn't know what to do while it's up there; and it's definitely elevated above its ability to function.'

'Right guys,' concluded Nellie, 'ah think you've all had your tuppence worth and this wee drawing room is getting warm and stuffy. Thanks for coming an' ah look forward tae some interesting feedback in your newspapers, plus the usual social media sites an' no doubt the telly. Noo, ah've got tae get on with looking after Scotland. That is sacrosanct. Thanks for coming. Please help yourself tae the refreshments in the next room, and don't overdo it if yer driving.'

'The Scottish Parliament is a place where visitors sit and watch MSPS straddle fences.'

BIG NELLIE NELLIS

CHAPTER TWO

Big Nellie's Inaugural Speech as First Minister

'PRESIDING OFFICER, FELLOW MSPS, it gives me dubious pleasure tae have accepted the role as the new First Minister of the Scottish Government.

'Ah have listened many times to your diseased minds as you have all spouted forth self-righteous crap. Your erstwhile smug delight at deluding your constituents with your half-baked, ill-thought-out bunkum has been a national disgrace fur too long. You are bereft o' what is good for Scotland. You have nae vision, nae principles and nae values. In short, you are nothing more than a bunch o' muppets.

'In this life folks can be doctors an' idiots. They can be scientists an' scruff. But if they're third-rate toon cooncillors who are more devoted tae their expense accounts like you lot, then they are mostly idiots and political pygmies – an' you lot take the biscuit. Anyone who has had the misfortune tae listen to your drivel will have realised that yer tribal pissing contests are only tantamount tae the product o' pathetic, egotistical ambitions an' monumental self-delusion.

'In this Parliament of deranged deadbeats, you have failed tae get your heads oot o' yer big fat posteriors for too long. Let me tell you, you unprincipled, fully paid-up anoraks an' tribalists o' minor consequence, that the tectonic plates o' this Parliament are about to shift.

'Be aware that the very demons o' hell will be unleashed on you all once ah get into ma stride. Ah will personally gut and fillet the lot of you. The halcyon days have gone. Your shenanigans are over. Your limited powers o' imagination cannot envisage the damage ah will do tae you dunderheids collectively and individually. Ah will specialise in political assassinations. There wull be rammies. Anybuddy who doesn't agree with me will be pensioned aff, heap pronto. Turning the other cheek is no' an option ah employ. As far as ah can see, you've all got the backbone o' a Tunnock's wafer. Nae class. You probably all sook the paper efter ye eat yer fish supper.

'You blame society at large, climate change, the gnomes of Zurich, the EU, plus Uncle Tom Cobley an' all fur your shortcomings. Finance, governance, health, justice and education systems plus transportation aw need attention. Young people feel disenfranchised. Your wheedling excuses are lamentable. Even your spin-doctors cannot whirl you oot o' it. Some of your parties have been rebranded, renamed, reorganised, modernised and merged... all a waste of time an' effort.

'Ah have already had a meeting with the Scottish Secretary of State regarding ma plans for this Parliament, and let me tell you he is another cretin who is nothing more than a pompous individual. A man who specialises in peddling mince. A glib, sanctimonious, self-serving wally.

'So let me make it clear to youse aw. Just forget the Barnett formula. You're now going to get the Nellie formula! This lady's no' for turning, apart from turning ye over on a spit.'

'Naw First Minister! Naw, naw, naw! Ye cannae possible say that,' interrupted Fraser MacLeod, otherwise known as Razzle Dazzle, Nellie's PA. They were sitting alone in the First Minister's office at St Andrew's House — an Art Deco-influenced building, set on the southern flank of Edinburgh's Calton Hill housing the offices of senior politicians at the Scottish Parliament, and around 1400 civil servants.

'Definitely naw, Minister,' he added shaking his head. 'You would be crucified, hung, drawn and quartered. Far too provocative. They would all think the Monster Raving Loony Party had got in. You have got to take it easy, First Minister. Calm down. Fool them intae thinking that you are sympathetic tae some of their policies. Softly, softly catchee monkey is what I say. Your opening speech, First Minister, should really be about setting out the legislative programme of this government, or a statement of government priorities over the coming term. You'll need to change it, First Minister.'

Nellie turned and looked at her PA, a pleasant man she had quickly learned to trust, middle-aged with a ready smile, and rugged good looks coupled with flopping fair hair and twinkling blue eyes.

'Ah know that, Razzle. Sadly you're right. But ah wid love tae let it rip. It would be rare fun to really shake

them up. The press would have a field day. Ah wid go down in history as having made wan o' the few honest political speeches o' aw time. A politician who told the truth; noo that would be something different, eh?

'Never mind, Razzle. Ah'll pit in a few different words so ah jist hope they can read between the lines; that is if any o' them can actually read. Now, pour me another wee swally, there's a good man. Oh, aye, an' here's another thing. Take a note tae get new blinds fitted in this office. Ah think they wans must've been here since the time o' that Donald Dewar.'

'Politicians are always correct.
Misinformed perhaps, inexact,
bull-headed, fickle, even downright
stupid... but never wrong. Aye, right!'

BIG NELLIE NELLIS

CHAPTER THREE

Squeaky Bum Time

'HELLO, DUDDY SPEAKING.'

'Hello there.'

'Yes, hello there. Who is speaking, please?'

'It's ehm, me.'

'And just who is me?'

'Neil. Neil Forbes.'

'Yes, Neil. You didn't sound sure for a minute. So what's the SNP's big problem today?' he chuckled.

'Let me tell you this is no laughing matter. My problem is really the same as yours. That Big Nellie. She's running riot. Does what she pleases. Someone who is always up to a bit of jiggery-pokery. The media love her and so do the electorate. She has got to be stopped. Put in her place.' The volume of Neil Forbes voice rose as he spoke.

'Well, I am all ears, Neil. You're sounding a bit desperate. For once we may be on the same side. Just what do you suggest?'

'What we need is a plan. You know, a concerted effort. Attack her with one voice. What do you say, Dud?'

Duddy looked around his office at St Andrew's House, at the same time wetting his lips with the long, thin tongue of a lizard hoping to catch an insect. A man with a well-shaped face of scattered freckles, high forehead and a mat of tight brown curls. Stiff eyelashes blinked over alert blue eyes behind silver-framed glasses which always gave him a perpetual slithering, hating sneer especially when he attempted to score cheap political points off all and sundry. Someone who usually kept his fingerprints off controversial issues associated with the governance of the country, and had already acknowledged to himself an intense hatred of Big Nellie. A pleasing smile now set about his lips.

'First of all my name is Duddy, not Dud, Neil. If you want my co-operation remember that or I'll be calling you Domestos, and I understand you don't like that. You are quite right, we need to do something but we would need to be ultra-careful. I must acknowledge though, funnily enough, my mind was running along the same lines. What we require perhaps is Nellie to be caught up in some sort of a scandal. For goodness sake, her background is still a bit of a mystery, isn't it. At the moment she's a vixen with the run of the hen-coop. There must be something we can zero in on. I'm getting freaked out, too, if the truth be told.'

'Nice to hear you telling the truth,' sneered Neil Forbes. 'The problem is, Duddy, if the Scottish media suspected we were involved in anything we would all be out of politics for ever. Go down in history along with Guy Fawkes.'

'Now, there's an idea,' smiled the Dud.

'Listen, Duddy,' warned Domestos, loving as usual the sound of his own voice. He was a man prone to

NEIL FORBES
SCOTTISH
NATIONAL
PARTY
LEADER

passing comment plus wind, much to the amusement of his opponents and the annoyance of those in the immediate vicinity. 'We have to be extremely careful. Only a few people should be in on this. As my old grandfather used to say, "three men can keep a secret if two are dead."'

He paused to consider the overall situation in his mind. Clearly Big Nellie did not enter political life as a pale and fragile rose. It had soon become evident to him that here was someone who was uncompromising in her homespun candour. When he and the other party leaders had realised what they had on their hands as First Minister, all had been incandescent with rage, especially as she continued to stoke the fires of controversy with brilliant blasts of excess directly cutting across their own ideological thinking and grassroots politics. Many of his party grandees, verbally mugged by Big Nellie, now seemed to have given up their hoo-hah and sat bereft in a trance like hyperventilating goldfish. This was punctuated by occasional bouts of resigned nodding, lower jaws jutting out, giving them the look of a bruised boxer, stubbornly distant, while grinding teeth so loudly you could almost hear it across the debating chamber as Big Nellie had the effrontery to throw out emotionally compelling commands like weapons of mass destruction. Yes, something desperate had to be done.

'We have a real problem,' Domestos continued. 'This woman is formidable. She defies convention. She is unusual on the spectrum of political reason. This will not be easy especially as she seems to have ice in her veins. To be fair, and it does hurts me to say this, she probably has the interests of the country at heart. Probably raises the Saltire every time she pulls up her knickers. So we need to get any plan of action absolutely right, otherwise she'll be all over us like a rash. I wonder who are the people we could include in this? What about Humph, the Tory guy?'

'Probably. She's made mincemeat out of him a few times so I can't imagine he's a fan.'

'And what about the Greens? Neon is a bit mercurial but might give us some ideas how to tackle someone of her own sex — though, by heavens, Nellie is certainly different from the rest. Neon has been walked over a few times by Nellie. But you know what they say, "hell hath no fury like a women scorned" and all that.'

'Mmm,' replied Duddy. 'I think that we should think this through carefully. We don't want any leaks. What about her PA Fraser MacLeod, you know Razzle Dazzle; I just wonder how loyal he really is, Neil?'

'I would forget about him. He's her closest ally. A bit of a twerp at times but he is her closest confidant. If she had a hip pocket, Razzle would live in it. In fact I think they may have something going, if you ask me.'

'Interesting. Now that's an angle I hadn't thought on.'

'Listen. What about discussing the whole thing after we have to listen to Big Nellie's weekly withering lines and general slaughtering at *First Minister's Questions* on Thursday?'

❋ ❋ ❋

The high-tech audio system of the Scottish Parliament's debating chamber ensures clear communication to MSPs, the students and visitors in the gallery, and to the millions who now watch the 'show' on television. Ratings are sky-high for a daytime programme and there is a repeat in the evening for those who missed it. It is now beamed to a number of countries and there has even been talk of a Big Nellie fan club, something unprecedented in Scottish politics. Nellie's Tweets are viewed daily by some twenty million twitterati, and her Facebook by a similar number.

First Minister's Questions take place every Thursday at 12.00pm. In the past it has been commented on that it lacked atmosphere and theatre, unlike the Westminster Parliament at Prime Minister's Question Time. It is now much changed to a lively affair with some commentators referring to it as 'Whollyrude at Holyrood'. As with all good variety shows there is a warm-up act in the form of various questions being put to Cabinet Secretaries and minor government officials on a variety of subjects.

At two minutes to 12.00pm, with everyone else seated, Big Nellie made her star-studded entrance to rapturous applause from the public gallery, which the Presiding Officer and stewards were unable to quell. Nellie — dressed in a black suit over a flounced, white silk blouse fastened at the neck with a silver broach covering her imposing bosom — was a picture of elegant perfection. Now it was time for the team captain to inflict pain on opposition MSP inquisitors with observations generously endowed with understated sarcasm — if they were lucky.

Nellie sat composed, like a batsman about to be called to the wicket to score a number of boundaries as the proceedings were opened by the Presiding Officer, Jeanie Cameron.

Presiding Officer: 'Brian Duddy to ask a question of the First Minister.'

The Scottish Labour Leader usually took great care with his choice of words, being a wheeler-dealer in subtlety, obliqueness and cynically petulant observations.

'Thank you, Presiding Officer. First Minister, perhaps you could inform us of any, shall we say, important engagements you have for today?' he sneered.

'Certainly. Ah will be involved in meeting various international captains of industry who have now been inspired tae

ORRDERR
HAUD YER
WHEESHT

JEANIE CAMERON
PRESIDING OFFICER

49

locate their companies to Scotland. They know we have a rich kaleidoscope of talent and skills readily available.'

At this pronouncement significant applause broke out in the public galleries.

Presiding Officer: 'Brian Duddy.'

'Oh, right, emm, quite good,' he sighed. 'Now, the First Minister has compiled a most interesting — to put it mildly — manifesto of proposals. Not only are they different from what would normally pass as shall we say, objectives for this new session of the Parliament, but they will clearly be extremely costly. Just how is the First Minister going to obtain the funds to support her manifesto proposals?'

Presiding Officer: 'First Minister.'

Nellie stood, arched her back and spread her fingers out like a cat briefly unsheathing its claws, before replying in a voice as sweet as cyanide.

'Ah wish to thank the Labour Party Leader for asking this question. Ma manifesto proposals have proved extremely popular with the Scottish public including the constituents that Dud, that is Mister Duddy, represents. Don't you worry, ah will ensure that they are properly costed oot, significant savings made elsewhere, an' the necessary funding provided.'

Presiding Officer: 'Mister Duddy.'

'That is a vague and idiotic answer, First Minister. This is a big issue,' he pronounced in tones of lugubrious self-righteousness.

Presiding Officer: 'First Minister.'

BRIAN DUDDY
SCOTTISH
LABOUR LEADER

'Don't mock me, ya wee nyaff or you'll soon be selling The *Big Issue*. Presiding Officer, in the short time ah have been in the Scottish Parliament ah have learned that keeping everybody happy at Holyrood is impossible. But pissing them aff sure is a piece o' cake as ah have just demonstrated tae this eejit. Don't worry, Mister Duddy. All my manifesto proposals will go through an' ah will expect your support, otherwise the support for your party in Scotland will be severely impacted.'

The Dud shook his head, appearing as snorty as a pinch of pepper. 'That is nothing more than blackmail, First Minister.'

'Mister Duddy, as First Minister of this wonderful country, it is my duty to provide the best possible benefits to all our citizens, even the ones who may have been foolish enough to vote for you. Ah intend to implement ma raft o' new measures. An', having read your own party's manifesto ah must say that it seems to have been cobbled together from a mixture of newspaper articles, official minutes, last election's manifesto, an' with a touch o' the Hans Christian Andersen thrown in, all adding up to a feeling of overwhelming indifference. The whole thing is worthless. You couldn't sell it in a pound shop!'

Duddy sat, finally looking cowed and submissive.

Next up to bowl was the Tory Leader, Alex Humphrey, a man who used to think he could match the First Minister with his bent for frivolity but was now extremely cautious. A court jester whose career path had peaked and was now erratic in the way he tried to belittle opponents by deflating and frustrating all proposals put forward. Really just a treacherous, dishonest and downright silly lightweight, always not quite saying what he meant during a career containing a litany of blunders and gaffes.

Presiding Officer: 'Alex Humphrey to ask a question of the First Minister.'

'First Minister, may I suggest that your slew of new policies could benefit from some discreet modifications which I and my colleagues would be only too happy to recommend to you. For instance your proposals do not give any indication on your, shall we say, "fine" thoughts regarding taxation,' he sneered. 'You may wish to expand your document into a more wide-ranging one. Funding is key to all new initiatives. Taxes are unfortunately necessary. Does the First Minister believe it is the duty of our citizens to contribute to the running of this country by paying their taxes with a smile?'

'Naw, cash,' stated Nellie. 'Furthermore, Mister Humphrey, ah will be most happy to consider any constructive suggestions you may have on this subject. Jist so you know my "fine" thoughts let me spell them out to you. Tax is a fine you pay for doing well and a fine is a tax you pay for doing wrong. Ah thought a highly regarded politician such as you would have known that.'

'First Minister,' replied Humph haughtily, 'thank you for your acknowledgement of my political standing. I must tell you I have the privileged position of knowing that when I walk down my local high street, all of my constituents acknowledge me.'

'Aye,' interrupted the First Minister, 'and like the rest o' your lot you would kiss babies an' steal their lollies at the same time. An' ah bet that when folks wave tae you on your local high street they don't use aw their fingers!'

'I will ignore that remark, First Minister. Now let me go on to tax. Taxation is important to the overall welfare of Scotland. It should always be carefully thought out. Louis xiv's finance minister once declared, "The art of taxation consists in so plucking the goose as to obtain the largest possible amount of feathers with the smallest possible amount of hissing." The First Minister should keep this in mind.'

'Thank you for your advice, Mister Humphrey, regarding geese and taxation,' observed Nellie. 'It is clear to everyone that you are just a silly plucker.'

Humphrey sat down, looking like a quivering wreck.

Presiding Officer: 'Diana Duncan to ask a question of the First Minister.'

Diana was seen as a bit of a pantomime dame having a flare for theatricality. This was emphasised by her generous thorax and the navy tights she continually wore which made her legs look like two throbbing varicose veins.

'Thank you, Presiding Officer. First Minister, as a woman would you agree with me that although many sporting institutions, such as golf and bowling clubs, are now allowing women to become members, it is essential that all clubs should allow women free access?'

ALEX HUMPHREY
CONSERVATIVE

'Absolutely, Ms Duncan, though ah suspect the real reason is that there are three centuries o' dirty dishes in the sink.'

'And what do you think, First Minister, about the equal opportunities bill for all sexes and ages?' she asked.

'Ah think it is vital, though you should understand the only reason they say "women and children first" is just to test the strength o' the lifeboats.'

'Very funny, First Minister,' she bridled. 'But on this very serious subject the female sex in Scotland is left trailing behind the male sex in a number of ways. It is not appreciated in this country that the pain of childbirth is the worst pain known to man.'

'You're a bit out there, Diana. Ah think you need to read some books on childbearing,' smiled Nellie. Sniggering could now be heard from the public gallery. 'Never mind, it would be pointless to make fun of you because it would take you the rest o' the day tae figure it oot.'

Wild laughter broke out amongst most MSPs and those in the gallery.

'Orrrderrr!' shouted the Presiding Officer and as the noise failed to die down an even louder shout of, 'Fur heaven's sake, wheesst!' came from 'Genie' Cameron. Gradually order was restored.

Presiding Officer: 'Now, Tom Smith to ask a question of the First Minister.'

The Liberal Democrat Leader was inclined to be

DIANA DUNCAN · GREEN PARTY ·
WEARING HER GOAT HAIR JUMPER
WITH THE PRETTY REPEAT NEEP MOTIVE

somewhat stroppy. Because of this he had committed political suicide a number of times causing support for him to plummet, leaving his party in the throes of a collective nervous breakdown.

'Thank you, Presiding Officer. First Minister, a recent paper issued by the Department of Health gives a health warning for Scotland that everyone should exercise more. Apparently one can die by doing nothing. What are you going to do about this worrying report? Other countries are taking this sort of thing seriously. Let me tell the First Minister, I should know as I have travelled extensively in Europe.'

'Aye, probably tae Torremolinos, Benidorm and Magaluf. Ah will ensure that this warning is widely reported to the people of Scotland. However, if you can die by doing nothing, there must be many MSPs here who are now worried sick.'

'First Minister, on a follow up point on health, should we not be doing more to encourage constituents to fill in their donor cards so they donate organs and brains to others? I would also advise the new First Minister that looking after constituents is a difficult business, not a flippant one. It is a life full of trial and error.'

'Aye, their trials and your errors, no doubt,' snapped the First Minister, adding further injury. 'Anyway, ah must say that ah admire people like you who wish to donate their brains. My only observation is that you should have waited until you died.'

'But, First Minister, what about waiting times at

A & E departments? What resources are you proposing to put in tae solve the problem of our population living longer?'

'Mister Smith, there is little discernible sense in that question. You have just proved my assumption regarding your brain.'

'First Minister, regardless of your mocking, I want to tell you that I am here today because I heard the voice of the people calling me to duty.'

TOM SMITH
SCOTTISH LIBERAL DEMOCRAT

'Are ye sure it wisnae an echo, Mister Smith?' quipped Nellie.

There was no comeback from Thrombosis Smith.

Presiding Officer: 'Neil Forbes to ask a question of the First Minister.'

'Thank you, Presiding Officer. First Minister, as you will be aware it is part of the SNP's policy to encourage all things Scottish. Should you not be encouraging more men in Scotland to be true Scotsmen and wear the kilt?'

'Absolutely. Though it will be a brave true Scotsman who will swing his kilt aroon in January,' smiled Nellie. 'Ah would put it tae Mister Forbes that he may well wish tae set an example in this respect.'

'First Minister, in addition, would it not be good that everyone should be encouraged to get out into Scotland's wonderful countryside and see what nature has done for us.'

'Totally agree, though ah'm surprised that Mister Forbes is making this point in view of what nature did tae him!'

Presiding Officer: 'Hugh Rae to ask a question of the First Minister.'

Hip Hip shuffled slowly to his feet. A man with a brick-coloured face and brain to match. Someone who would have done credit to a creature from the Neolithic age. Hip Hip turned to face Nellie like a weary Saint Peter at the pearly gates interrogating yet another sinner trying to wheedle his way into heaven.

'First Minister, you have in your manifesto a proposal

that all MSPs should meet a minimum educational standard. Are you not therefore preventing many of the population from taking part in our democratic Parliament?'

Nellie stood up, an exasperated look on her face. 'It's very simple, Mister Rae. We require the best brains to run the country. Furthermore we must encourage education. You know what they say, give a jackass an education and what you will get is a smart ass… and we've got a number here today. Ah'm excluding you.'

Further damage to the contestants was prevented by the Presiding Officer calling time on the bout. All listeners of a nervous disposition then gave a sigh of relief that no further damage could be inflicted by the First Minister.

❀ ❀ ❀

The presence of the two politicians went unnoticed in a discreet corner of the busy Bella Italia restaurant, near to Edinburgh's Waverley Train Station.

Neil 'Domestos' Forbes had arrived first. He had waited ten minutes for a table then kept it while nursing a cappuccino for a further 20, leaving the waiting queue unhappy at this individual monopolising a table and not even ordering a meal. He kept his head down and read *The Times* before Brian Duddy eventually slid into the chair across from him.

A dark-haired waitress took their order. Both ordered

Spaghetti Gamberi with prawns, chilli and garlic – a house favourite – along with mineral water. After all, they had to keep their minds clear to address this sensitive problem. Between strangulated mouthfuls they conversed in hushed tones.

'Seriously, Brian, we must take some sort of action. This cannot possibly be allowed to continue. She is making fools of us all; she outfoxes everyone. The woman is Marmite, some of our MSPs hate her and some now think that's she's the best thing since sliced bread.'

'You're right. Mind you, that sounds a bit like a sandwich, Neil.'

'Brian, our reputations are being seriously undermined. I am emotionally exhausted. We are both reasonably intelligent individuals, so surely we should be able to come up with some sort of idea how to oust this Nellie Nellis. Anyway, is the woman left or right wing? She just seems to continually have her own agenda. We cannot be complacent about this. I'll be honest with you, sometimes I would rather undergo root canal treatment than face her, it's that bad.'

The admission was surprising as Neil Forbes had a reputation as a man who sometimes was brutal. It was also said of Domestos that he really liked to act posh and usually had one of his flunkies beside him who carried a spare hankie and cash on their leader's behalf. Regrettably he had an unfortunate jaw-line which allowed his upper front teeth to hang out to dry as he spouted his words leaving him looking like an unctuous Co-operative undertaker. As he ate food today this became somewhat pronounced.

The Dud nodded his head in agreement. 'The problem is, Neil, what to do? As politicians we have got to keep umpteen plates spinning on sticks aloft all at the one time. Surely you can come up with something? You're supposed to be sharp. I heard that at one time you applied to the Law Society to become a lawyer. What happened? Did they reject your application because your mother and father were married?'

'Very funny. Listen, this job is difficult enough and now we have this new-fangled First Minister to contend with. Right across the political spectrum everyone seems to be at her beck and call. And she is so blooming popular with the public at large, they all seem transfixed. At times she can be so personable and plausible. Did you see the graffiti on the front of the Parliament Building? 'Big Nellie Rules' and 'Nellie doesnae shilly-shally… gets stuck in!' And they just love all this innuendo and cut-throat wit. The media coverage is ridiculous. Only last week there was a BBC crew in the Parliament Building and, when I asked, I was told they are doing a documentary on the woman. I ask you, have either of us had a documentary made about us? And we've been in politics much longer than Nellis.'

'It's no use whinging, Brian. I think that one of the other problems we have is that you have to admit she is quite a good looking woman, and that makes her even more newsworthy as far as the papers and their male readers are concerned. But you're right. Basically we need to do some background checks on the woman. You've heard the rumours of her family in Glasgow being involved in criminality, haven't you? That may or may not be true. We really need to dig up the dirt on Nellis.'

'For a minute there, Neil, I thought you were going to say you fancied her or that she would make a good page three model, eh? I know you have a reputation for liking the ladies. One of my people said women don't trust you too near and men don't trust you too far. But on the question of her background, surely she was thoroughly vetted before she was allowed to stand as an MSP. They're quite strict about that nowadays, you know.'

'Let me butt in here, Brian. You are maligning my reputation. Most men fancy the ladies. I am totally trustworthy. Are you telling me that you are squeaky clean? Everybody has skeletons rattling in their cupboards.'

'That's interesting. So what's yours, Neil?

'Don't be funny. Let's forget about us. We need to concentrate on "you know who". Can we not hire a private detective, or somebody like that, to sniff around?'

'Mmm. Not a bad idea provided we don't fall into the trap of breaking those stringent privacy laws we passed.

But we need to find somebody who is totally reliable and discreet. Any leakage and the media will be on to us. Our careers ended. No doubt it would cost a few bob but if it worked, great! Got any suggestions?'

'Well, I used a private snoop when I thought my Margaret was having an affair. And she was. Proved quite reliable, though a bit of a maverick. Did the business. Got all the necessary info for me, and saved me thousands with the settlement.'

'Sounds as though we may have the man, Brian. Who is he and what will he charge?'

'He's not unreasonable in his costs, Neil, and we can pay him cash, just in case there is any comeback. He goes by the name of MacSnape. Appears at first glance to be laid back but he most certainly isn't from my own experience. Looks a bit sinister at times, in fact reminds me of Adolf Hitler.'

'Well, old Adolf was a bit of a dictator so I just hope this fellow can work to our instructions, or should I say command. I assume we'll go 50:50 , Duddy. Anyway we may be able to put it through expenses. We'll think of something to charge it against.'

'Fine. I'll see if I can get in touch with him again. Right, I think we should be on our way. Some nosy parker might just see us together and think that we make strange bedfellows, then make a call to the newspapers. You can't be too careful nowadays. You pay the lunch and get the receipt. Ah'll keep you up to date on progress when we play in the medal on Saturday morning. If you are still stressed about this Nellie thing I will even buy you a restorative gin at the 19th hole. How's that for a cross party agreement?'

'Aw they MSPs have one philosophy…
"You cannae try me for blaming!"'

BIG NELLIE NELLIS

CHAPTER FOUR

Go Ahead, Make My Day

IT STARTED WITH the sounds of the alarm ringing in her brain, then she was conscious of her throat like barbed wire.

Nellie thought she had swallowed razor blades. Her forehead felt hot. Then she discovered she didn't have a temperature or there was something wrong with the thermometer. She shook it vigorously but the bloody thing showed normal. Typical government issue, she thought. Then she sneezed. A further thought occurred. She knew exactly where she got this cold. It was that meeting she had with 'Wonga', George Woods, Convenor of the Finance Committee to discuss her financial plans for the Parliament. He had continually blown his nose throughout the hour that she and Razzle had spent with him.

Things had not gone well at the meeting. As she had commented to Razzle afterwards, 'By any measure of tedium yon is off the scale. Couldnae pull a fiscal lever if he tried. Wants to stay "revenue neutral". Ah ask you, what does that mean? He needs to help me get this country out of neutral and intae top gear. Nothin' but wind and piss in a tie.'

'Otis! Are you up yet?' Nellie shouted to her erstwhile

son who lived with her in the small accommodation area at Bute House. 'You'll be late for your shift!'

Otis had been the result of a short time Nellie had spent in the USA many years ago. No mention was ever made of the father and no one had ever had the guts to ask her. Otis was now in his early 30s, tall, confident, loved the girls and was a bit of a handful even for Nellie, so when she got the First Minister's position she insisted he live with her. Keep your problems close, she had rationalised.

At least he had got a job in Edinburgh. Razzle's brother-in-law had managed to get him a job with the taxi and courier company which he worked for. On his courier's bike with his black leathers and long greasy hair, Otis now zoomed around the capital delivering she knew not what. What she did know was that he used his job to great effect when it came to women. His bright blue eyes, gleaming smile, raffish neckerchief and Arai helmet seemed to work wonders with the opposite sex. At times his Kawasaki bike had as a passenger some besotted bike chick who usually ended up with him in a night club or even the First Minister's residence, much to the consternation of Nellie and the Bute House officials.

'Ah've spoiled that boy,' thought Nellie for the umpteenth time. 'Get up, Otis,' she shouted again. 'Aan' get those socks o' yours into the laundry basket. They're mingin!'

'But, Mum, I hear you sneezing. I think you've given me your cold.'

That was another problem with Otis. He was definitely a hypochondriac. He had stated he was allergic to wheat and dairy and now pasta was a forbidden fruit. He had decreed that his decaffeinated filter coffee must only contain the merest smidgen of semi-skimmed milk. Recently he had gone for patch tests only to return triumphant that new exciting allergies had been found. For a month thereafter he seemed to eat nothing more than salad and rice cakes.

And now any colds quickly became man-flu transmuting quickly into a virus, which he interpreted as double pneumonia deep in his chest.

The trouble was that he had proved imperious to irony or sarcasm, even although Nellie now referred to him as a 'Fisherman's Friend junkie'.

'Get up an' get to work!' she remonstrated again, her voice somewhat hoarse and feeling brittle from her cold, and just managing to keep her displeasure in check. 'Take one of your famous Fisherman's Friends an' you'll be right as rain.'

Mind you, she had to admit that when he finally appeared he was somewhat pasty-faced and his half-shut eyes were red. 'Here, Otis, get this hot tea down you. If it was last thing at night ah would dish you oot a medicinal whisky toddy.'

'Well, Mum, you don't seem to have to wait until night to have some of your "medicinal" whisky. Anyway the sugar in the drink might give me false highs.'

'Oh, for heaven's sake! Listen, ah'm no' driving

around on a motorbike so a wee drink wouldnae hurt me. Ah'm in the back o' a ministerial limo.'

'You're always getting on to me Mum.'

'At the moment you're being a bit o' a pain in the butt tae me.'

'Okay, but I don't think I will be able to work today with this cold. And if you look out the window it's raining. Could you phone in to Dispatch and tell them I'm ill?'

'No way, Otis. You'll just need tae be a brave fellow for once in your puff. With great difficulty ah got you that job. Anybody else would be happy to be running around the capital delivering packages an' picking up girls the way you do. Anyway, you're the only person ah know who takes terminal colds.'

'Very funny, Mum. It's probably you who gave me it,' he said accusingly.

'Might be, and ah know who gave it to me. What ah do know is that ah thought you would have been in a profession by now rather than the casual work you seem to go in for. So let me put it this way, Otis. Get your erse over that door an' into the rainy streets o' Edinburgh where an undistinguished career is clearly stretching ahead of you. An' while you're at it get a nice girl, marry her an' get me some grandweans!' She followed this up by a dismissive gesture with her hand to signal that he should leave.

With a sniffle, a sneeze and a rheumy glance he was gone. Thank heavens, thought Nellie. Ah've enough to be getting on with trying tae run Scotland never mind an errant son.

She looked at her watch. There was a BBC Scotland radio phone-in she was scheduled to participate in this morning. According to Razzle she would have a slot at 9.45am. There was a loud knock at her door and her faithful PA entered.

'Good morning. Five minutes to go, First Minister.'

'Right, ah'm ready,' she sniffed.

'You're ready, First Minister? You sound dreadful. That's some cold you've got.'

'Tell me about it, Razzle. The listeners won't recognise ma voice today. It's that deep they'll think it's Gordon Brown.'

'Well, First Minister, if I may be so forward, can I give you some advice? Please don't get stuck in the way you normally do at some of these callers. They're voters, not MSPs. Be your usual cocky self by all means, but without putting the heid in if they try to get you wound up. No doubt some of the callers will have been put up to it by individuals in the Parliament, you know what they're like.'

'Probably. Well, tae be fair ah got you tae phone in a few months ago tae say whit a great job ah wis doin' and how ma manifesto was fresh and challenging.'

'You're right, First Minister. The only problem was that most o' the listening MSPs recognised ma voice and raised the issue at a Question Time.'

'An' ah jist told them straight that it wis a damn

disgrace that someone should go on air an' impersonate ma PA,' laughed Nellie. 'Accused the hale jing bang lot o' them o' underhand dealings. Actually got us some good publicity on the despicable tactics of opposition MSPs at Holyrood.'

The phone rang. Razzle answered. 'It's the BBC producer, First Minister. Thirty seconds till you go live.'

'Fine, Razzle. Noo, jist you sit doon and listen.'

'Thank you for agreeing to join our programme today, First Minister,' came the voice of Isobel Smyth, the phone-in presenter for the day. 'I know you have a busy, demanding schedule. Your first caller is a Sydney Maither from Dundee.'

'Hello, First Minister.'

'Morning, Sydney,' Nellie croaked.

'They say, First Minister, that politics is the second oldest profession but it does seem to bear a close resemblance to the first. What do you think?'

'Well, Sydney, ah wouldn't want to argue with you. After all, you seem to have an intimate knowledge o' at least wan o' these professions. Ah suppose you could say that both give themselves in their own way fur the benefit o' mankind.' Nellie turned away from the phone and raised her eyebrows as if to say, 'What a stupid question!'

'Our next caller, First Minister, is Sylvia Grace from Bathgate. Sylvia, please make your comments to the First Minister.'

'First Minister, it is essential for the future of this

country that young people are properly trained and educated. So why, when it comes to education, do politicians provide a rich stream of inane and plain daft changes to an already pretty good system?'

'Listen, Sylvia, ah'm assuming you're in the teaching profession. It's key that our education system remains vibrant, though when we measure ourselves against some other countries we need tae do more in maths and physics. But ah also want tae encourage some o' the clever young people o' this country tae get into politics an' push for further improvement in education. In the meantime ah'm doing my best to encourage the existing dinosaurs to move on.'

'So, First Minister,' said a mollified Sylvia. 'Would you describe yourself as someone who is for change and who is a Scottish patriot?'

'Of course, Sylvia. I'm continually defending Scotland against this Scottish Parliament!'

'Thank you Sylvia. Your next caller is Wayne Kerr from Glasgow.'

'First Minister, what are you doing to stop people getting high street loans? And what are you going to do about loan companies who are targeting children an' getting them into debt? It's ridiculous. You are doing nothing about this!'

'Listen, Wayne. These companies are merely copying what the Government has been doing for years. It's called the Student Loan Scheme. And by the way, you're obviously well named.'

'First Minister, your next caller is John Leitch from Aberdeen.'

'First Minister, I am phoning to say that your approach to politics is refreshing. Before you came on the scene the Scottish Parliament was like an abandoned spaceship after a fruitless mission to find intelligent life. Are you finding the job exciting, First Minister?'

'Thanks for your observations, John. Ah must tell you that if ah was any more excited ah'd be a threat tae the environment. If you enjoy any job and feel you are making an improvement then you are motivated.'

Nellie looked up to see a smiling Razzle. The bugger had obviously done a good job and got this 'John' person to phone in.

'First Minister, your next caller is...' suddenly Nellie was hit by a bout of coughing and sneezing. She blew loud and hard on a paper handkerchief quickly stuck in her hands by Razzle.

'Sorry about that,' she stuttered. 'As you can hear I've got a bit of a cold. Right, what is the next question, please?'

'It's Kenny from Selkirk here, First Minister. Your sneezing is perhaps appropriate to my question. What is your position on the NHS? Would you privatise parts of it?'

'Absolutely not, Kenny. The National Health Service is vital tae ensuring the health of our population. Ah will personally fight aff any attempts tae move it into the private sector. Mind you, Kenny, it would be good if they could do something about ma rotten cold.'

At that Isobel Smyth the host came on to say that she much appreciated the First Minister taking part, especially when she was obviously somewhat under the weather.

The producer then spoke to add her appreciation of Nellie's participation and the line went dead.

'Well, First Minister,' observed Razzle, 'you at least managed to deal with that despite your cold. That will be appreciated.'

'Thanks, Razzle, for arranging the phone-in and keeping me straight,' said Nellie, her hoarse voice worsening. 'Ah've got to say you are more than just ma PA. You're a real pal.'

Razzle looked at her keenly. 'And you're a bit special to me, First Minister.'

'Good. In that case get me a hot toddy. Stick plenty o' the gold stuff in it.'

'If you really want anything in life you need to work hard for it. Oh, that reminds me, ah didnae check ma lottery ticket oan Saturday night.'

BIG NELLIE NELLIS

CHAPTER FIVE

The Investigation

ALTHOUGH WELL PAST ten o'clock at night, the bar in the Balmoral Hotel seemed to be an open house for some, flirting over their whiskies and cocktails. It was here that Brian Duddy, Leader of the Scottish Labour Party, stood contemplating his pending appointment, while holding his double gin and tonic.

Privately he acknowledged that the drink was in order to provide a little Dutch courage for the meeting arranged for later on. Yes, he was nervous.

His thoughts were interrupted by a slap on the back and there stood an acquaintance he would rather not have met, tonight of all nights.

The man was lean and tall, slightly crooked in his posture and with some rugged features including a scar leading from his mouth to his chin giving him a leering grin. The dark eyes flashed.

'Evening, Brian. Good to see you. What brings you here tonight?' The words were delivered in an unsmiling monotone.

Immediately Duddy was on his guard. Henry Spiro was well known for his investigative journalism. A man with a nose for scandal. A man well bred, well dressed, well heeled and, well, a pain in the arse.

'Just having a snifter before setting off for home, Henry. And what about you? Anything interesting you are following up on at present?'

'Not really,' said Spiro looking directly into Duddy's eyes. 'Mind you, I would like to do something on that Nellie Nellis. Now there's somebody of major interest. Always in the papers. High profile. So, come on and dish the dirt on our esteemed First Minister. You must hate the way she addresses you all. What about another drink, Brian?'

'No thanks. This one's fine. I've soon got to be on my way. My driver is just round the corner,' he lied. 'Anyway, you will not get anything on Nellis. She always seems to have all the angles covered.'

'Come on, Brian, now there must be something you can give me on her? I can't believe you don't have some tiny wee suspicion at the back of your mind on some of her activities. Eh? This could be to both our benefits, you know.'

'Sorry, old chap, but nothing comes to mind,' he said quickly finishing off his drink and placing the glass on the bar. 'Must go and inspect the plumbing before I set off. See you.'

And with that Duddy made his way to the gents. Once there and in a cubicle, he took out his mobile. 'Hello, is that you, Neil? Good. Look, get yourself a taxi and meet me at the top of Leith Walk in a quarter of an hour. Okay? Yes, I know it's raining. I'll be under my golf umbrella. Bye.'

※　※　※

The taxi sped through the relatively quiet streets of the Edinburgh night to an area of town set in a dreary, unexotic suburb that the two MSPs would not normally consider visiting, even in daylight. It was now after 11.00pm and quite dark and raining. Ideal for the purpose of their visit.

'Driver, just drop us on the corner here,' instructed Duddy.

As the vehicle sped off Duddy confided that Adolf's office was actually in a lane some hundred yards ahead. 'You see I didn't want that cab driver to have any inkling of who we're seeing or what we're up to.'

The pair duly set off, hiding from the rain and any inquisitive members of the public beneath Duddy's golf umbrella.

They found the entrance in a dark alleyway leading down from the lane in question. Beside a nondescript door an array of entry buttons presented themselves beneath a lurking CCTV camera.

Before pressing any button they dawdled for a moment, looking round to ensure they were alone. Satisfied, Duddy pressed a buzzer then duly identified himself. A loud click summoned their entry and the door sprung open. A spiral of ill-lit echoing stairs led to a further flight of poorly lit stairs, which in turn brought them to a small landing leading to a worn metal door upon which the name "A. H. MacSnape, Private Investigator", was badly painted. A further buzzer was pressed and eventually, after a number of locks were undone, a face appeared.

'In ye come, gents,' rasped the voice. 'Sit doon,' he added, pointing to two worn buttoned leather armchairs.

The room was amazingly higgledy-piggledy, cluttered with various road maps and files apparently flung haphazardly around. The only light was from a green baize desk light which showed that Adolf was a relatively young wiry chap with a mop of suspiciously dark hair, wearing a moustache reminiscent of the Austrian housepainter. A determined glint showed in his perceptive eyes, and there was a suggestion of cynicism from an ironic tilt to his mouth.

'It's not often I'm found in the office at this time, gents, but for two such distinguished persons as yourselves I hope I can help. You said this was to be a totally confidential affair with only the three of us involved. Now, am I right?'

'Absolutely, Mister MacSnape.' Duddy started nervously, his eyes focused on a paperknife Adolf had picked up and was now fiddling with. 'This is an

MAC SNAPE

(ADOLF)

extremely sensitive matter. Can you reassure us that this conversation plus any subsequent investigations will remain totally confidential? Nothing, absolutely nothing, must leak to anyone unless we authorise it.'

'Most certainly.' Adolf failed to stifle a sigh. 'That is fundamental to my business, gents. It says on the door "Private Investigator" and I totally understand the meaning of the word "private". If I don't do things purely to my clients' instructions then that is the end of this business, and knowing some of my clients, that would be the end of me.'

'This discussion is not being recorded?' queried Duddy.

'Absolutely not, sir.'

'Well, the person I, rather we, want you to investigate is,' – and he hesitated, almost frightened to mention the name – 'Nellie Nellis.'

At that a broad grin spread over Adolf's face. 'Isn't she just something else, eh? Certainly got you lot on the rack.'

'I would disagree with you there, Mister MacSnape, but it is certainly true that she is popular with, shall we say, certain sections of the population.'

'You can say that again. Not a bad looking woman, too for her age,' relished Adolf. 'Can be a bit of a doll at times. Maybe eye-candy for the older man, eh? Quite a few eyes turn when Nellie appears.'

'Aye, and a few MSP stomachs as well, Mister MacSnape,' said Neil. 'I hope that your apparent enthusiasm for Nellis is not going to be a hindrance to what we want?'

'Gents, if you have the money then I will have a nosy around and dig up dirt on anybody, and I assume that's what you're after? Mind you, you've got to admit she's a bit of a Rottweiler, eh?'

'Well, I wouldn't quite put it as crudely as that,' intervened Neil. 'We are here merely – shall we say – to do what is best for our country.'

'Of course,' replied Adolf with a smile. 'Okay. So exactly what do you want me to do?'

'Simple. A fair and honest assessment of her and her background, Mister MacSnape.'

'No problem. But surely the police, MI6, Taggart, Rebus and everybody and their granny will have vetted her up and down before she got the job?'

'I am sure that will have been the case, Mister MacSnape,' observed Duddy. 'But a man with your skills and instincts, and no doubt contacts, can search in other areas that have perhaps not been covered.'

'Okay, gents, give me a starter for ten. I understand the brief. What can you tell me about Nellie Nellis?'

In the relative gloom of the office the MSPs exchanged glances.

'Not a great deal,' ventured Neil. 'The truth is she's

an enigma, a mystery. We know she has a son who is presently living with her in Bute House. We know that Nellis comes from Glasgow, and there have been whispers her family have in the past been up to no good. Also, that she spent some time in the States, apparently living in the New York area.'

'Sounds as though I may have to do quite a bit of digging and travelling on this one, gents. Could be costly. Just so there should be no misunderstanding, I will require two grand up front and my daily charge will be three hundred quid, plus expenses, of course. And given the sensitivity of me investigating the First Minister of Scotland I want it all paid in cash; small denominations; used notes.'

Again the MSPs exchanges glances.

'How long will all of this take, Mister MacSnape?'

'Impossible to tell. I also have a few other inquiries at present which I will need to continue with. Got to keep all the clients happy, gents,' he smiled, revealing the need for overdue dental work.

More furtive glances were exchanged between the MSPs. It was clear they were thinking along the same lines. Duddy cleared his throat.

'If you drop everything else you are doing Mister MacSnape, we will make it five grand up front.'

The sleuth raised his eyebrows, and a bony hand suddenly stretched across the paper strewn desk.

'Shake, gents. I'll start tomorrow. *Once* I get the money, you understand.'

'Okay, but you understand we need to be kept up to date on your progress, Mister MacSnape.'

'Don't worry. I'll keep you up to speed.'

'The major problem with the acoustics in the Scottish Parliament Building is that no matter where you sit you can still hear some of the speeches.'

BIG NELLIE NELLIS

CHAPTER SIX

On Desert Island Discs

'RIGHT RAZZLE, tell me what's on ma plate today,' asked Nellie of her Personal Assistant as they sat in her office at St Andrew's House.

'Well, First Minister, first of all you have Wonga in at 9.30am to talk about local government funding'.

Nellie looked over at Razzle from behind a desk which displayed a profusion of government papers, old editions of *The Scotsman*, a framed photograph of Otis sitting astride a motorbike, and a laptop.

'Oh, that consummate professional wee git. Great start to the day ah must say. That man is useless. Cannae count an' thinks slower than anybody ah know. Ma granny had a gall stone that moved quicker than yon. So what else is there?'

'You've got the Presiding Officer, 'Genie' Cameron, at 10.00am. Wants to talk to you about some complaints from MSPs that you are being, well, sort of unkind in your observations to them in the chamber at *First Minister's Questions*. Deputy First Minister Alaska McAlpine will join us for that one.

'Unkind? Unkind tae that bunch o' incompetent zombies!'

'Also, First Minister, there's been a phone call from the BBC.'

'Tell them ah've paid ma licence, Razzle.'

'Naw, First Minister, the phone call was from BBC Radio. They would like you to take part on *Desert Island Discs*.'

'Aye, nae bother. Ah'll look through ma CDs. Ah'll enjoy doing that. Remind me when ah've got a minute tae think up a list. So, when am ah on *Desert Island Discs*, Razzle?'

'It's a bit short notice, First Minister, but they were wondering if you could do it next week? Your Friday diary then is relatively light, and I could reschedule a number of meetings. A wee trip down to London might be a nice change. You'd only be away one night.'

'Fine, Razzle, but ah'll need to think o' Otis. Ah don't trust him alone in Bute House. He'd have a wild party wi' half the girls in Edinburgh swinging from the chandeliers.'

'First Minister, excuse me but it's now 9.30am. George Woods – you know Wonga, the Convenor of the Finance Committee – is probably outside. May I suggest we let him in?'

'Aye, Razzle. Let's get it over with. You know, he's jist an old fool on steroids. You can always tell: wide hips, long arms and a thick brain.'

Wonga tentatively entered the office. Sure enough he did have wide hips and long arms. He also had floppy grey hair, a delicate pale face, death-ray halitosis and the limpest, dampest handshake. He winced as Nellie shook his hand.

CONVENER OF FINANCE COMMITTEE
GEORGE (WONGA) WOODS

'Good morning, First Minister,' he said cautiously.

'Good morning, George. Please sit down.'

'Ah wanted to talk to you, First Minister, about local government funding and new Council Tax bands that some of the local councils are proposing.'

'Well, you know, George, it's up tae local councils if they want bands or orchestras,' grinned Nellie.

'Very droll, First Minister. As you know the funding for the regions has been approved, but the Councils are all moaning that it is insufficient. You have insisted that all wheelie bins be uplifted every week. They are saying they will need further funding to do that.'

'Listen, George. You're not talking "wheelie bins" you're talking "pure garbage",' she fumed. 'Okay, give it to them. Ah must have ma manifesto implemented.'

'But where will we get the funding, First Minister?'

'That's up to you, George. You're the money man. You've got gazillions in your budgets. Go an' have another look at your sums, an' then tell me how you are going to manage this.'

'But the other political parties will not be pleased.'

'Tough. There is not wan o' them MSPs has a grip on economics. Only last week ah heard Hip Hip Hugh Rae statin' that, if he was in charge, he would ensure that everyone would get an above average salary. They havenae a clue.'

'Well, is there nothing that you can tell me, First Minister, on the action I should take?'

'Ah'll just give you wan bit of vital information before you go, George. Yer flies are open.'

A flustered Wonga hurriedly rose and made for the door, adjusting his clothing as he went.

'What a wally,' exclaimed Nellie. 'That guy fudges everything. Cannae make a decision. Needs a spot o' fiscal waterboarding if ye ask me.'

'Right, First Minister, it's time for Cameron, the Presiding Officer to see you. Murdo 'Alaska' McAlpine will be coming in, too.'

'Okay, Razzle, wheel them in. Ah cannae be bothered wi' thin-skinned bureaucratic types like 'Genie' Cameron, an' ah'm certainly no' going tae summon up an apology for whatever offensive remarks ah'm alleged tae have made.'

Genie the Presiding Officer followed by Alaska, entered Nellie's office. She was clearly as nervous as a feral cat. They both sat down.

'Good morning, Genie,' smiled Nellie. Genie flushed at the use of her nickname. 'Ah believe you wish to give me a reprimand?'

The bespectacled Genie had short hair, was significantly overweight, and arrayed in a jacket not unlike a chainmail vest.

'Well, First Minister,' began the Presiding Officer, 'Not a reprimand as such, but I have been approached by various MSPs who have, shall we say, been somewhat unhappy at the... outer limits of forthright statements you have made in the debating chamber.' Genie's plump fingers jerked and trembled as she explained her situation using various chops in the air with flattened hands, a gesture often used by her in the Parliament. She then gave a sudden start, shook her head, leaving her jowls wobbling.

'Listen, Presiding Officer,' countered Nellie. 'Ah must tell you that the media an' public feedback to ma "forthright statements" has been positive. Too many o' oor mealy mouthed politicians don't deal wi' situations head on. Ah do. Unless the court o' public opinion goes against me in this respect, then ah will continue tae address situations frankly.'

At this Genie touched her chin feverishly. Her lips pouted.

'You must remember, First Minister, that it is not just "Joe Public" who have human rights; MSPs have them, too. What do you think, Deputy First Minister?' she asked, looking desperately at Alaska for support.

'Well,' began Alaska uncertainly. 'I am sure that the First Minister is probably, emm, well, sort of right.'

'Ah'm definitely right, Deputy First Minister,' corrected Nellie with a growl. 'And let me tell you that, tae qualify for human rights legislation, MSPs have tae be human!'

'Is this your final position on these concerns?' asked an even more nervous Genie.

'It certainly is!' replied Nellie, staring directly into the Presiding Officer's blinking eyes before flapping a dismissive hand toward the door, through which, a moment later, Genie retreated.

'Thanks for your support, Murdo,' said Nellie sarcastically, and Alaska too quickly left.

'Well, that put Genie's gas at a peep,' observed Nellie. 'And see that Alaska, whit a waste o' space that wan is. Now tell me more about this BBC *Desert Island Discs* programme.'

'Okay, First Minister. Well, basically every week a distinguished guest, and you're obviously one, is asked to choose eight pieces of music. You need to let BBC Radio 4 know your choices a couple of days before the programme. It's Jenny Wilson who is the interviewer, so she's Scottish, which will make you feel at home. And another thing, you have to pick your very favourite disc out of the eight. You are allowed one luxury on your island, so you need to have something in mind. You are also asked which book you would like to take with you, and in addition to the book selected they automatically give you *The Complete Works of Shakespeare* and the Bible.'

'No problem, Razzle. Sounds like a bit of fun.'

'It's more than a bit of fun, First Minister. You could say it's a status symbol of having, in some way, made it.'

'How many people have actually been on *Desert Island Discs*, Razzle?'

'Over 3,000, First Minister.'

'This is no deserted island, Razzle,' said Nellie giving vent to one of her full throated laughs. 'Sounds as though they don't even have an immigration policy.'

'It's a great opportunity to project quite a broad-based, rounded image of yourself.'

'Listen, Razzle, ah don't want a broad base. Ma bum is starting to look fat in most things.'

'Just so you know, First Minister, your life and career will also be discussed in between the music.'

'Mmm. Well… okay, then. Let's see how it goes, Razzle.'

❀ ❀ ❀

Nellie's first thought, as the plane landed at Heathrow, was she needed a fag.

The BA flight from Edinburgh was full. Nellie was accompanied by Razzle Dazzle, and two rows back sat Ralph, a security officer.

Most of the flight time had been occupied with Nellie signing autographs for passengers, posing for selfies, and listening to their various tales of woe, whilst basking in their appreciation of her different approach to Scottish politics. She had thoroughly enjoyed the flight, especially the two double whiskies, although she had a fear that her coffee would end up in her lap and ruin the new outfit bought for this special occasion. Then she relaxed as she remembered the show was on radio.

Within a minute of landing Nellie switched on her iPhone. She quickly scanned the list of 50-odd emails, including a copy of one sent to Razzle from the BBC driver informing them that their limo was waiting in the VIP area.

Nellie was seated by a window on the port side of the aircraft overlooking a wing. There was the usual crammed rush for lockers baggage as the engines powered down. Razzle and Ralph retrieved the carry-on bags. A flight attendant made an announcement informing everyone that there would be a short delay before the cabin doors opened. Razzle looked at his watch in frustration. 'Hope it's not too long, First Minister, otherwise we might be late for the recording schedule.'

Nellie finally stood up in the aisle and looked around. A couple of passengers back, there was a man who was studiously making an effort not to look at her. Looks like Adolf Hitler, she thought. Is it my imagination or have ah seen him around the Parliament Building?

Five minutes later Nellie, Razzle and Ralph were finally able to shuffle down the aisle to the door, and up the ramp following the 'Way Out' signs.

The driver had been waiting quite a while, but was deferential and courteous to the First Minister, even when she insisted on having a cigarette before entering the vehicle.

Razzle told the driver that it would be greatly appreciated if he could drive as fast as legally possible as they were tight for time.

Forty-five minutes later they drew up at Broadcasting House, the impressive iconic hub of the BBC with its external piazza and Art Deco design. Again Nellie lit up. Standing beside her, Razzle got the downdraft of her cigarette smoke. Filthy habit, he thought.

A young blonde woman in her late 20s wearing a fashionable trouser suit and a clip-on smile approached, introducing herself as Jenny Wilson's assistant. If they would kindly follow her she would take them through security and up to the green room.

The BBC Radio 4 green room proved to be relatively small but was clearly well stocked with nibbles and booze.

'Can I get you a drink, First Minister?' asked the assistant.

'Have you got Glenmorangie?'

'Yes, we have.'

'Let Razzle, my PA, pour it if you don't mind. He knows the measure ah like.'

As Razzle rose to get her drink, he whispered, 'Remember, you had a few on the plane down, First Minister. Every MSP will be listening to this programme. So you need to watch what you say.'

Nellie shot him a stinker of a look as if to say, 'I can hold my drink.' This was soon followed by the clunk and rattle of ice cubes pinning against her glass, and the throaty glug of single malt.

Only ten minutes elapsed before it was time for the recording. The studio that Nellie was shown into was tiny with a glass window through into the production team. Jenny Wilson, an attractive woman with a pleasant smile to match, rose with a warm welcome and handshake.

'First Minister, I have really been looking forward

to this episode. I was so delighted when you accepted, although I'm afraid we didn't give you much notice.'

'Very happy to be here, Jenny. Ah've been looking forward tae this, too,' smiled Nellie in her usual devil-may-care manner.

'First Minister, we are all set to go. Please make yourself at home.'

She indicated a seat beside a table with various microphones sticking out of it. 'It would be helpful if you put on your earphones. I must say that I was intrigued by your choice of music, First Minister, so I believe this will be one of our most entertaining episodes.'

'Ah hope so, Jenny. Ah must say ah've had great fun making up my mind on the songs.'

The green light on Jenny's desk turned to red. Nellie looked and saw the producer giving a thumbs-up sign through the glass. The familiar music of the programme's theme tune 'By the Sleepy Lagoon' began to play, evoking thoughts of a paradise island.

'Hello, I'm Jenny Wilson. My castaway this week is a lady who has made quite an impact on the political scene with her rigorous, uncompromising style and libertarian approach to the freedom of speech. She is responsible for the development, implementation and presentation of Government policy, and constitutional affairs for Scotland. Quite a job description. Welcome to *Desert Island Discs*, Nellie Nellis, the First Minister of Scotland.'

'Delighted to be here, Jenny.'

'First Minister, you must have been amazed that you were appointed straight into the weird and wonderful world of politics with the top position in Scotland, especially after such a short time on the political scene?'

'Ah was, Jenny. Weird and wonderful is bang on. Mind you, when ah looked around at some of the weird individuals who might have been appointed, then ah could understand how ah got the job.'

'Have you found it challenging and exhausting, First Minister, with all this sudden responsibility?'

'Naw, Jenny. The fact is that ah'm totally motivated to introduce ma key new policies which will improve the lot of the Scottish people. Government is all about principles, and ma principle is never to act on principle to get things through the Parliament.'

'Now, First Minister, I believe that you were brought up in the Castlemilk area of Glasgow; perhaps not the most salubrious part of the city.'

'Jenny, ah believe that is one of ma major strengths, because with my childhood and background, ah feel ah can better relate to oor population's needs.'

'Right, First Minister, it's time for your first piece of music.'

'Jenny, this song takes me back to ma childhood. Perhaps to a poorer but simpler way of life. One of the problems of today is that children no longer seem to play outside the way we did many years ago. Running around, playing games used up a lot of energy for masell and ma friends, and it also seemed we were forever hungry. If you lived on the top floor of a multi-storey flat as ah did, then it was long way from the ground floor back up tae your home for something to eat. And if ah recall correctly the lifts seemed to be continually oot o' order. So my first track is, "The Jeely Piece Song", you know, all about mothers wrapping up jam sandwiches and flinging them out window to their weans below. Made a jammy mess, but it was very tasty. I think the song was written by Adam McNaughton and sung by Matt McGinn.'

Nellie mouthed the words as she heard the opening strains of the selection coming through her earphones, and when she looked up Jenny appeared to be giggling.

'Well, that was certainly somewhat different from the norm, First Minister. And it was catchy, too. Now moving on, I believe that you have caused quite a furore with your approach to various political issues, much to the chagrin of some of your political opponents.'

'This is very true, Jenny. As you know in any walk of life there is rivalry. Ah'm sure you find that in your own sphere of work. Certainly, in the political field where every decision is challenged, then you do have a lot of opposition. Ma manifesto has been much appreciated by the majority o' oor electorate, but some of oor MSPs have been critical of aspects of bills ah have presented at Holyrood whereas they should be open to change, an' be able to transcend petty party politics.

'Every aspect of ma life, even ma clothes, has come under scrutiny. However, when you examine some o' the moans, then ah am reminded of the words of ma second song. It's the Jeanie Riley number, "Harper Valley PTA" which was written by Tom T. Hall. In it Mrs Johnson comes under criticism from the local parent teacher's association for her lifestyle an' clothes. Ah just love the way Mrs Johnson socks it right back tae her critics. Magic!'

The catchy song was heard through Nellie's earphones, and her face lit up with a smile and her toes tapped in time.

'Interesting, First Minister. Perhaps there's a message in the lyrics for your political opponents and critics?'

'There is indeed, Jenny. Ah may have been on the political scene for just a short time, but it hasn't taken me lang tae get tae know where all the dead bodies are buried. The Scottish Government is not a team game, you know. It's a loose fiefdom of warring clans.'

'First Minister, what's your next choice?'

'In fact the discussion on clothes fits in nicely with ma next choice. This time ah've chosen one for all the ladies. You know sometimes the opposite sex can take us for granted, Jenny, an' here's me, the sexiest politician oan the planet according tae some o' the comments ah get oan Twitter.' Nellie stopped and gave a hearty laugh before continuing. 'This track is, "Did I Shave My Legs For This?" by Deana Carter. Ah'm sure all o' your women listeners regardless of age will totally get this. You get all dolled up for a man an' he lets you down. Then you ask yourself, did ah shave ma legs fur this?'

Nellie's head moved in time to the music and a smile crossed her face.

'I understood that one completely, First Minister,' laughed Jenny. 'Now, moving on. As most people will know you stood for the Scottish Parliament as an independent candidate with no formal party backing. And here you are as First Minister. With no support by the other parties do you sometimes feel you are vulnerable?'

'Ah'm not vulnerable in the least, Jenny. Certainly the requirements of the position are demanding but that is jist great because ah thrive on the challenge. The other parties voted for me in the first place to be First Minister, so if they don't support me when necessary that is a clear reflection on them. An' ah have ma trusty aide, Fraser MacLeod, who is most helpful in helping me get around the maze o' Parliamentary procedures.'

'But surely being at the top in any organisation is a lonely job, First Minister?'

'It could be, Jenny. But the truth of the matter is that ah'm enjoying it, an' that is half the battle. Cut and thrust is right up ma sleeve. The big difference between me an' other politicians is that ah thrust ma dagger in the front no' the back.'

'Now I've already touched on your reputation as

a formidable opponent, First Minister. I have heard that you are, in effect, now slaughtering most of your opposition.'

Nellie laughed. 'Let me tell you, Jenny, that ah have never killed anyone... so far. But ah do read many political obituaries with pleasure.'

'First Minister, your life must be just one busy meeting after another.'

Nellie laughed. 'Just so you know, ah never hold a meeting until ah've first dictated the minutes, Jenny.'

'Now I see how you operate, First Minister,' smiled Jenny. 'Can we talk a little more about your life? Although you were born in Glasgow I understand your family moved to the United States. How did you feel about that?'

'To tell you the truth, at the time ah didn't have any say in the matter. America is a great country and many Scots have flourished there. The sad thing is that Scotland's biggest export has been its people. And that brings me tae ma next piece of music which is "Letter From America" by The Proclaimers. The lyrics ah'm sure perfectly reflect the sentiments o' many Scots.'

The sentimental words made a pensive Nellie nod in keeping with the words.

'As a Scot myself, First Minister, these lyrics do indeed make me somewhat sad. Now, let me ask you a little more about your time in America. Ah assume you went to school there?'

'Aye, Jenny, the family lived in upstate New York.

The schooling was, shall we say, tough. Ah certainly enjoyed growing up in America but ah guess there was always something missing, an' that was Scotland.'

'What about American politics? Were you interested in the political machinations over there?'

'Oh, aye. My father was big on politics and ah guess his interests became mine. Ah certainly remember attending a number of political gatherings. They were great; full of razzmatazz and fun. An' there was the same old intrigue, manipulation and rabble-rousing that we have in Scotland.'

'First Minister, I won't ask you which side of the political spectrum you favoured in the USA, but can I ask why you eventually opted to return to your homeland?'

'Two things, Jenny. Sadly ma father died and a year later ah found masell pregnant. So ah quickly opted to return to ma roots,' explained Nellie.

'Now, First Minister, by the sound of it your life has mostly been spent in large cities. How will you manage to cope on this desert island? You know, build a hut, and grow vegetables and catch fish?'

'Jenny, ah've always managed through the problems in my life. Ah'm assuming that this desert island is somewhere warm. As much as ah love Scotland, ah don't fancy being marooned oan some wee island aff the Outer Hebrides with no central heating.'

'Right, First Minister, now let's have another track. What's your next choice?'

'Jenny, although I don't always admit it, ah quite like most men, even some Scottish politicians. Now ah don't want anyone to misinterpret my next choice but you will understand, as a woman, the attraction of this number. It's "Secret Love" written by Sammy Fain and Paul-Francis Webster from the musical *Calamity Jane*,' she added coyly.

As the track played Nellie's eyes seemed to go all sentimental and a sudden tear appeared in the corner of an eye. She pulled herself together. Must be the booze, she thought.

'So, First Minister, you find yourself back in Glasgow. How did you find the contrast with America?'

'Well, Jenny, the great thing about the Scots is that we are a friendly, outgoing bunch. We make people welcome; we usually try tae help each other. Americans are also great, but they are busy rushing aroon all the time trying to make a buck. So ah've loved being back in the old country. The social scene is also grand. Ah guess ah finally realised that Scotland's really been everything ah ever had an' valued. An' this is reflected in ma next piece, "Caledonia", written by Dougie MacLean an' sung by Amy MacDonald.'

Nellie's head moved thoughtfully in time with the sentimental theme of the lyrics.

'Very fitting, First Minister. Now I wanted to talk to you about how you are managing to drive through some of those very interesting proposals in your manifesto. For instance you wish to change the voting ages, have MSPs clean your Parliament Building, have minimum educational standards for MSPs etc. You don't have a majority, and obviously you will require an agreement with some of the other parties to implement your proposed bills. So, you must find it difficult at times.'

'That's true, Jenny. What ah do have though is the apparent support of the majority of the Scottish electorate. Ma political opponents are aware of this, an' acting against some o' the manifesto items puts them in a poor light with the population at large. However, it is also true that ah do have ma ups and downs but that is the ultimate distillation o' life in politics. And ah'm most certainly not easily dissuaded when ah set my mind tae something.'

'So, First Minister, what would you say makes a great political speech?'

Nellie thought for a moment before replying. 'Ah would say, Jenny, that it is one where you cannae tell if the politician is lying, an' that nobody can prove that they are lying.'

'Interesting definition, First Minister. Now I do know that, despite your overwhelming appeal to most, some of your opponents do say cruel things about you. I may be a little forward in saying this but I read recently on Facebook that someone actually wrote you were like Miss Piggy, from The Muppets. How do you cope with comments like that?'

'All ah can say, Jenny, is that as ah recall, Miss Piggy

was a no nonsense character, so ah will take it in some ways as a compliment. And, believe you me, ah have been called much worse.'

'Now, First Minister, it's time for your seventh selection. What's it to be?'

'This song, Jenny, says it all. Ah'm in Parliament for the people o' Scotland. So in that vein ah have chosen Van Morrison's "I Will Be There".'

The unique voice of Van Morrison was heard singing his popular song.

'Now, what kind of person are you really, First Minister?' asked Jenny. 'If you were to sum yourself up, how would you describe Nellie Nellis?'

'Ma political opponents may mock at this but ah feel ah'm not just tough, but where necessary, helpful and warmhearted. Ah do admit that ah do not suffer fools gladly. But ah do feel that ah have a sense of humour, an' ah certainly need it. Now, excuse me, Jenny, ah assume this is being recorded so can you stop and edit it?'

'Of course, First Minister.'

'Then I'd like to change ma final song. Ah had selected "I Will Survive" by Gloria Gaynor. But assuming ma suggested replacement is in the BBC Record library ah'd prefer it.'

'So, what's it to be, First Minister?'

'It's "Nellie the Elephant".'

Jenny laughed heartily. 'Fine, we'll get that changed.'

Within a couple of minutes there was a thumb up

from the producer indicating that they were ready to resume.

'Now, First Minister, what is your final piece of music?'

'Certainly the words of this song will appeal tae some of ma rivals, but they should note it may be sometime before ah come to pack up ma trunk and leave our Parliament. It's "Nellie the Elephant" written by Ralph Butler and Peter Hart. That'll give a few folks something to think aboot. Actually a circus song is not inappropriate fur the Scottish Parliament the way some o' they clowns there juggle figures around.'

Nellie's and Jenny's heads moved in time to the catchy music.

'Never had that on *Desert Island Discs* before, First Minister. It's definitely a first. And if I may say so you will certainly be remembered for providing such a varied and interesting selection.'

'Well, Jenny, hopefully ah have not only entertained your listening audience but given some o' them something tae think aboot.'

'And now you have to select your favourite number from the eight selected, First Minister.'

'Jenny, ah'm trying to envisage myself on this desert island. Lush, blue skies an' warm. So there ah am lying on the beach enjoying the peace an' quiet apart from the gently lapping waves. Then ah think of all the people in Scotland who are not so fortunate. So, to remind me of the old days – and to be fair they were actually good old days – ah will choose the "Jeely Piece Song".'

'Now one luxury item for your desert island, First Minister.'

'What ah want, Jenny, is a never-ending supply of Glenmorangie malt.'

'No problem. I'm even sure we could build a distillery for you on your island. Also, as you will be aware, we give you a copy of the Bible and The Complete Works of Shakespeare. In addition, you are allowed one book of your own choice. What will that be?'

'Ah will need a book that reminds me o' both the cheeky humour o' the Scots an' their many pearls of wisdom. So ah have selected the book of Scottish sayings, *Gonnae No Dae That!*'

'First Minister, I have got to say it's been a real pleasure having you on the show. Thank you, and enjoy your desert island.'

The red light was suddenly replaced with a green one.

'I must say, Nellie, if I may call you that,' laughed Jenny, 'I couldn't help but hear the mischief in your voice during the recording. Thank you so much for taking the time to come down to London,' and she gave Nellie a warm hug.

'Nae problem, Jenny. It's been lovely tae meet you.' And with that Nellie was duly shown back to the green room.

Immediately a harassed Razzle, shaking his head so vigorously that dandruff seemed to be expelled by centrifugal force, whispered in her ear. 'Pssst, First

Minister, I told you not to have any more drink, First Minister. All the other party leaders will just love the "Nellie the Elephant" bit. In fact I can see the attention-grabbing headlines right now.'

'Stuff them, Razzle. Jist get me another wee goldie.'

'The Scottish Government should change its emblem from a thistle to a condom: condoms give a sense of security while actually screwing you.'

BIG NELLIE NELLIS

CHAPTER SEVEN

A Working Majority

THE LARGE COMMITTEE room was one of six meeting rooms in the Parliament Building, and gave off an executive air with its unusual ovoid shaped table set around what resembled a drained swimming pool. It was capable of seating up to 30 people with most positions having an integral microphone sticking out from the table surface. A further 20 seats were available around the walls.

All the principal players in the Parliament were there. Everyone, that is, apart from the First Minister. Then, just as the assembled throng were starting to check their watches and speculate that she was perhaps having a last crafty fag, in came Nellie followed by the faithful Razzle Dazzle. Nellie looked around the room then took some time settling into her chair at the head of the table. Extracting a handkerchief from her handbag, she loudly blew her nose then placed the bag on the floor before looking around once more. All eyes were on her.

'Good morning, everyone,' smiled Nellie. 'Thanks for coming tae this vital discussion. The subject o' this morning's meeting, as you are all aware, is ma excellent manifesto proposal that all MSPs should take a day each week to carry out maintenance and cleaning o' this building. So, who's going to start off?'

Nellie looked around. Deputy First Minister Murdo 'Alaska' McAlpine sat on her right hand side, his eyes apparently now fixed on some papers in front of him. The Tory Leader, Alex 'Humph' Humphrey, coughed twice and then settled back in his seat, clearly wishing someone else would kick-off the discussion. Green Party Leader, Diana 'Neon' Duncan was looking for something in her handbag. Everyone else's eyes suddenly seemed to be intently studying parts of the walls or taking an interest in the traffic outside.

Then came the voice of Tom 'Thrombosis' Smith, the Lib Dem Leader. Everyone sat up.

'Emm, First Minister, this proposal of yours, or should I say this very unfair part of your manifesto, is totally outwith the remit of MSPs.' Tom's voice had an edge to it. He was either angry, nervous or both. Nellie's steely eyes on him probably didn't help. 'You see, First Minister, when candidates initially came forward for selection as MSPs, they expect to give 100 per cent of their time to look after the welfare of Scotland. There is absolutely no hint that anything like this would be required of them. MSPs of every party can be very busy at times, both with their work here in the Parliament and with their constituency surgeries. To suddenly demand that they give up a vital day each week merely to look after this place is beyond the bounds of reasonableness, and totally against the spirit of normal democratic government.'

Clearly emboldened by the Lib Dem Leader's

MURDO McALPINE
DEPUTY
FIRST MINISTER

statement, James 'Ben' Nevis, a quietly spoken man of austere bearing, who seemed to wear authority like a favourite coat, was quick to get in his tuppence worth. 'Surely you see, First Minister, that MSPs were not sworn into doing such menial work. Their key area is devising and introducing policy. You wouldn't expect your driver to carry out a service on his vehicle, now would you?'

'No, but ah would expect him to give it a clean and polish,' countered Nellie smoothly, a pasted smile on her face, while swinging in her chair in a manner deliberately calculated to annoy.

It was at this stage that the SNP Leader, Neil 'Domestos' Forbes came into the fray, his face long and grave.

'First Minister, we all heard you recently on *Desert Island Discs*. Now I don't want to be rude, but your choice of "Nellie the Elephant"' — and a titter went round the table at this — 'perhaps gave the impression to the listeners that you can trample over everything in your road. This part of your manifesto cannot just be pushed through. It is… just unacceptable.'

Much nodding and various 'agree's' were heard. All eyes then turned apprehensively to hear Nellie's response.

Nellie swallowed back the response she really wanted to make. Her initial reply was surprising.

'Mister Neil Forbes is quite correct,' the First Minister said with a wry smile. Suddenly the tension in the room slackened at this unexpected statement from Nellie,

JAMES **NEVIS** CONVENER OF ECONOMY
ENERGY AND TOURISM COMMITTEE

only for it to be immediately ratcheted up again.

'You said, Mister Forbes, that MSPs don't like this idea. But, by heavens, the general population certainly do. Politicians of all parties suffer from a very poor public image. You know this. "Only in it for what they can get out of it" is one of the many derogatory remarks continually made about us. The public think of politicians as the good, the bad and the ugly. If you fail to support this, they will know you as merely good-for-nothing. In the latest poll over 80 per cent of those contacted liked the idea of MSPs getting their sleeves rolled up and actually – dare I say it – working. Now, ah realise that in order to get this through the Parliament it will require support.

'So let me spell it oot to you because ah can see the newspaper articles already in ma mind's eye,' continued Nellie in an annoyed tone. 'They will list the names of those who were actually prepared to work for Scotland and save over two million pounds each year, and those who voted against it and are merely in it for an easy ride. "Nellie the Elephant" doesn't require to lead a charge on this one. The general public have already done so.

'The court of public opinion is, as you know, one that dishes out particularly severe sentences, with no appeal. It's up to you. You will need to apply joined-up thinking and logic to this one. You all know ma feelings on the matter. So, let me leave you to your deliberations. The sparring is over. Just let me know the final decision in order that ah can call a press briefing.'

Nellie took her time looking around at everyone around the table, a grim smile on her face. Sniffing, her handkerchief appeared once more as she again blew her nose, then she arose and made a slow dignified exit, followed as usual by her PA.

Outside the door Nellie said, 'Listen, Razzle. Go and get us coffees. Ah'm having a ciggy.'

Ten minutes later both were seated at one of the many bay offices found in the midst of all the odd cubby holes, nooks and crannies available to MSPs.

'I don't think they'll go for it, First Minister,' observed Razzle quietly, his face serious. 'Show that lot a sand dune and they'd stick their head in it. Best you can do is tell the press you are deeply saddened and disappointed at the poor support you've had. You know, allude to MSPs not being really interested in helping Parliament save money.'

'Don't you believe it, Razzle,' said Nellie with a wicked smile. 'That lot know which side their bread is buttered on and this is now a political hot potato. Tell you what, 20 quid says they agree. An' for heaven's sake stop calling me First Minister when we're oan oor tod. Ma name's Nellie.'

'Okay, emm… Nellie. I'll take yer bet. Sadly, the easiest 20 quid I'll ever make,' he said, running a nervous hand through his lush thick hair.

'Good, now what else have we got on.'

'Well, I was going to have a quiet word with you about something, First Minister, sorry… Nellie. It's probably nothing but on the other hand it could be serious. It's best that I whisper this to you,' he said moving closer to her. 'As you know my brother-in-law is a taxi driver. He was telling me that he picked up two politicians recently. Turns out it was Brian Duddy and Neil Forbes.'

'Doubt if he got a decent tip from that pair,' smiled Nellie.

'Don't know about that. But he reckons they were up to no good.'

'Going to wan o' them sauna places, eh?'

'No, Nellie.' Razzle tapped his chin thoughtfully. 'Jimmy, that's the brother-in-law, is the nosy type, so once he'd dropped them he parked his cab round the corner. He saw them disappearing into some alley. He nipped over and saw a dim light on in an attic. It transpires it's the office of a guy who is a sort of private detective.'

'Interesting, Razzle. But it's probably got nothing tae do wi' me.'

'You could be right, Nellie. Jimmy was chatting away to one of his mates regarding this investigator fellow. It turns out he's apparently a dead ringer for Hitler.'

'Eh!' Nellie's eyes narrowed. 'Are you sure about this, Razzle? Because that bugger was on our plane when we went to record *Desert Island Discs*.' she murmured. 'In fact ah'm sure ah've seen him around somewhere else. Yer right. These two sleekit numpties are at it. Obviously come to some "wink wink" agreement on this. Who can tell what thoughts have been percolating through their disturbed minds? Talk about the vagaries of human brains. They're a pair o' schemin', connivin' wallies. Ah'm goin' tae gut and fillet them!'

'Listen, Nellie. Perhaps the best thing would be if you were to challenge them? Put the shitters up them. Say you're going to the press.'

'They're goin' tae get a ton o' grief sure enough. But not right away, Razzle. Keep yer hair on. An' it's nice hair. Ah need to think this over carefully.'

'Well, it's a concern, Nellie. They're probably looking for skeletons in your cupboard.'

The First Minister shot him a look. 'Aye, an' there's plenty o' them, Razzle, that you don't know about.'

Their coffee was sipped slowly and in silence as they contemplated the situation. What was the best way to tackle this unexpected development?

Nellie thought back on her life. Where would this investigator search? Glasgow or perhaps even the States? She needed this like a hole in the head. Then she came to a sudden decision.

'Listen, Razzle. We need to get our retaliation in first. Ah would bet more than 20 pounds that these two buggers have not exactly led whiter-than-white lives themselves. But first we must keep this to ourselves. Switch off your brother-in-law so he doesn't gossip any further. Tell him that their visit to this Hitler person was definitely nothing to do with the Parliament. He's already chatted to a mate, so tell him to make sure he doesn't talk to anybody else or every Tom, Dick and Harry will know.

'Now, what ah'm going to do is get that pretty useless lump o' a sniffin' son o' mine oan the job. Otis must know Edinburgh inside out by now so hopefully he can put that knowledge to good use for once. Let's see what he can come up with when it comes to finding something oan Duddy an' Forbes an' even Mister Hitler. Let him earn his corn for once. Protect his old mother frae her enemies, eh? Once ah get any naughty stuff on them we can then have a session with our two friends.'

It was at this point a Parliamentary Clerk appeared.

'Sorry to disturb you, First Minister, but the group in the meeting room were wondering if you would rejoin them?'

Nellie and Razzle looked at one another.

'Okay, thanks, tell them ah'll be along shortly,' replied Nellie calmly.

She turned to Razzle and smiled. 'Rustle us up another couple o' cups, okay. Ah'm goin' fur another ciggie. That lot can wait for half-an-hour or so.'

Thirty-five minutes later Nellie and Razzle re-entered the meeting room. It was immediately noticeable that many individuals were red faced with flustered looks, some with dead-eye stares were slumped in their seats, and all of the men had removed their jackets. Some faces displayed fury, dismay, and perhaps defiance – it was hard to tell.

Nellie took her time taking her seat, deliberately

smoothing out her skirt and crossing her legs. She smiled demurely at the group. 'Okay, let's have it, boys and girls.'

Everyone turned and looked at Brian Duddy, the Scottish Labour Leader. Duddy cleared his throat, tugged nervously at his tie, and looked to the ceiling with obvious disquiet as if seeking divine guidance.

'Well, First Minister, we have had what I would say was a very full debate on this. I must now tell you that there is considerable opposition to your proposal. I think you already gathered that.'

Duddy stopped for effect and looked at Nellie who had turned to face him, her expression impassive. Before continuing, the Dud searched the anxious faces around the table for support. All shared a chilly politeness with a few sly glances being exchanged.

'Let me quickly get to the conclusion of our debate, First Minister. We finally had a vote, and it was unanimous. We cannot support your proposal of MSPs working a day each week on the maintenance and cleaning of this building.'

All looked at Nellie. Her eyes flicked over Duddy. She said nothing.

Duddy coughed, cleared his throat, and then looked around again before continuing. 'However, a counter proposal was put forward by myself, First Minister, that perhaps half a day each week could be acceptable to the parties. This was voted on, and finally agreed by one vote.'

All eyes went to Nellie. Her demeanour hadn't

changed. Not a twitch, no tapping of fingers, no change of her colouring. There was a silent pause while they awaited the inevitable outburst.

Instead, a huge smile appeared on Nellie's face and there was a note of amusement in her tone.

'And the bill to reflect this will be supported in the Parliament?' she enquired with eyebrows raised.

'Yes, First Minister.' A number around the table nodded, though some sat clearly unhappy at the prospect.

Nellie rose, 'Fine. Glad you guys are finally gonnae get tae work, even if it's only half-a-day a week!'

The assembled MSPs remained sullen and silent as Nellie and Razzle slowly left. It just wasn't their day.

Abruptly Nellie stopped outside the meeting room. Razzle looked quizically at her, then quipped. 'Now remember, that's 20 quid you owe me, Nellie.'

'Naw, Razzle. Jist ten. Ah wis half right. To tell you the truth ah'm absolutely shocked the buggers actually went for it. They bottled it!' Nellie allowed a grin of pleasure to spread across her face. 'Ah jist stuck it in ma manifesto in the first place tae liven it up. Ye cannae possibly have MSPs doin' cleaners and contractors oot o' jobs. The unions would go mad. Business would lose oot, an' then there's Health an' Safety tae think o'. Ah didnae even think they would even get as far as seriously considering it. Ah thought they would dismiss it oot o' hand, feel good about it, then be more supportive o' ma real manifesto proposals.

'So listen, Razzle. Jist you go back in there right now an' tell that bunch o' numpties that as they only partly supported this potential opportunity to demonstrate their absolute commitment to the Parliament, on reflection ah have decided tae drop their half-hearted support. Tell them ah'm really bitterly disappointed.'

'Okay, Nellie, I'll do that,' smiled Razzle. 'But do you know what the real problem is for them even voting for a half day?'

'No. Whit?'

'They're shit scared of you!'

'People used to vote for the party that would do most good. Now they vote for the one that'll do least harm.'

BIG NELLIE NELLIS

CHAPTER EIGHT

Dirty Pool

S T GILES' CATHEDRAL is the historic city church of Edinburgh. With its famous crown spire it stands on the Royal Mile between Edinburgh Castle and the Scottish Parliament Building.

At the heart of the cathedral is the sanctuary with the holy table and pulpit, surrounded by four massive pillars which support the tower and steeple. There are various aisles within the cathedral and it was on two of the end pews, deep into the building, that the two politicians sat.

Although it was a pleasant day outside, the atmosphere in the cathedral was on the chilly side. Looking around they saw some people lighting candles while many worshipers were kneeling to pray. A number of tourists sauntered down the aisles taking their time to look at various monuments and plaques.

Brian Duddy and Neil Forbes glanced down at their watches. Adolf was not on time.

'Sorry ah'm late, gents. Held up in traffic then ah couldnae find a parking space,' Adolf's voice suddenly came from directly behind them. 'Don't look round,' he instructed. 'We can talk like this.'

'Was this *really* the best place to meet, Mister MacSnape?' whispered Neil. 'Mind you, if you don't mind me saying so, the area your office is in is not exactly the *avant-garde* of Edinburgh sophistication.'

'Yer right. But this place here is perfect. Ah use it a lot. Sometimes even have a wee word wi' the Almighty.'

'So, what have you found out so far, Mister MacSnape?' asked Duddy impatiently.

'Not a lot. Been through in Glasgow fur some days. The subject, ah won't use the name, seems to have a lot o' loyal support there. Nobody really prepared tae spill the beans on anything. Apparently the subject had an uncle who wis a nasty piece of work. In and oot o' the clink, he was, but there wis no apparent contact with him whatsoever. So the link with organised crime doesnae stand up.'

'That's very disappointing, Mister MacSnape,' said Duddy with a frown. 'Are you basically saying that after almost a week you have found out nothing?'

'Virtually nothing. Ah did tell you that the subject would have been well checked out already, didn't ah? Paid all taxes on time, never in debt, everythin' clean as a whistle, in fact a good citizen tae all intent and purposes. Seems tae have been hard working in the factory where the subject worked. Quite a responsible job, too. Actually well respected. And then bringing up the boy as a single parent. Really quite commendable, ah say.'

'That may well be the case, but that is not what we're after, is it?' observed Neil Forbes, his voice clearly unhappy. 'Are you saying we are just wasting our money?'

'No, no. Ah'm o' the opinion there is something. In fact there's bound tae be a chink in the armour somewhere. Just haven't got tae it yet. I've followed her a number of times, including to London, then was nearly knocked down by a motorbike in Charlotte Square driven by some young idiot with a half-naked woman on the pillion. The trouble is the subject is driven around in a ministerial car. Also a security officer trails around everywhere after the subject; and as for that PA o' the subject, ah think they're umbilically attached.

'Ma instinct says the answer's got tae be in America,' continued the sleuth. 'Ah feel it in my bones. Ah've now managed tae get hold o' an old address in White Plains, New York, so ah can take it from there, assuming you two agree.'

'Okay,' a resigned Duddy sighed, turning to look for confirmation at Forbes, who nodded silently. 'See what you can find out. We've got to do something. This can't go on.'

'Fine, gents. Okay, ah'll leave you for now. Dinnae worry; ah'll give you regular reports on ma progress. Now ah suggest you give it a few minutes then you can both leave the cathedral. Cheers, gents.'

Some time later, as Neil Forbes and Brian Duddy came out of the cathedral into daylight, a tall man of crooked gait and with a scar on his chin stepped forward. 'Hello, boys,' he smiled.

Both recognised Henry Spiro immediately. 'So, what little scheme are you two up to?' Spiro grinned. 'Praying for guidance on how to deal with your First Minister perhaps, eh?'

'No, no,' blustered Forbes. 'Just thought it was time we did the touristy bit of Edinburgh for a change.'

'Aye, that'll be right,' chuckled Spiro. 'Did you have to hire a private detective to assist in this bit of culture seeking?'

'I'm sure we don't know what you are talking about.' Duddy protested.

'Let me put it this way. I have made a living by following my nose. You may recall our meeting in the Balmoral Hotel recently, Brian. Well, my nose was twitching that night, so if you two had looked out of the back of your taxi you would have seen my Jag. So, please don't kid me on that you have not employed the services of my Mister MacSnape.'

'*Your* Mister MacSnape?' they both echoed.

Spiro put on a smug face.

'MacSnape has been very useful to me in the past with various leads on stories,' laughed the journalist. 'So you may as well let me in on the action. I'm going to find out anyway, boys, one way or another. And if you think on it, I might just be of some help to you in spreading any muck!'

✦ ✦ ✦

'Right, Otis, ah've a wee job for you.'

'Is there money in it, Mum?' asked Otis as he stood in the small kitchen in Bute House sipping a vitamin C drink.

'Listen, all you seem tae think about is women, money and your health. For once ah'm gonnae give you an opportunity tae do something useful for this family.'

'This family! It's just you an' me, Mum,' sighed Otis, 'you never ever told me who my father was.'

'Be quiet, and listen, you! This is important. You like the Edinburgh scene. You are always up to a bit of nonsense. Well, if you don't do this wee job, ah could be oot o' ma job an' you would be out o' our digs,' threatened Nellie. 'It would be back to Glasgow for us. Ah'm still trying to placate some of the officials here after the party you had that time when ah wis in London on *Desert Island Discs*.'

'Okay,' sighed a resigned Otis. 'Whit is it I have to do, Mum?'

'Right. Put that drink down and concentrate. There's a private investigator that apparently has been given the job o' diggin' up the dirty oan me.'

'What! Why? Who's put this investigator on to you, Mum?'

'Good question. Ah think it's a couple o' the party big chiefs. Brian Duddy the Leader of Scottish Labour and Neil Forbes, the SNP Leader. They know they cannae beat me in the Parliament so they're now up tae playin' dirty pool.'

'But how can I help? Do you want me to knock them off? Anyway, what do they look like?' asked a confused Otis.

'Watch the Scottish Parliament on Holyrood TV or

BBC Parliament on the telly and you'll soon see who they are, Son. And naw, you cannae knock them off. That would really put me down the proverbial. Now you listen to me, Otis. You know Edinburgh well so that's a big help. Razzle has done a wee bit of initial investigation and he thinks the investigator's name is MacSnape. It wull be easy for you fur this fellow looks like Adolf Hitler. Ah want you to follow him, dead easy on that supercharged chariot o' yours, and find out what he's up to. Also, tell me when he meets up with these two comedians, Duddy and Forbes.'

'But ah've never met Adolf Hitler, Mum.'

'Of course no' ya daft dope, but you'll have seen plenty o' photos o' him. He's wis the wee fellow who started the last war, and let me tell you, sunshine, ah'm gonnae finish this war as the winner.'

'Maybe I should buy a tank and blast him to kingdom come, Mum!'

'Good idea, Otis. Blast them all if you like. But, knowing you you'd probably miss. Listen to me, Son. You're always pleading with me you cannae go to work because you've got some world-shattering, incurable illness. The only wan you've not had is housemaid's knee an' no doubt you're working on that. So, what ah'll do is phone your boss an' explain you're a bit under the weather an' you'll no' probably be in this week. Then you can go off an' see whit oor friend Hitler is up to.'

'But I'll not get any money, then. I'm on a zero hour's contract,' moaned the bold Otis.

'Don't you worry ma wee boy, ah'll pay you. An' if you come up with something of significance ah'll give you a bonus. But,' Nellie warned, 'if you don't ah'll give you a clout. Find out where this investigator fellow is going, and then use your initiative. God help us.'

'Aye, and what's the bonus I'm going to get, Mum?'

'Well, there are two. The first one is we stay in this nice wee flat for the next few years. The second one is ah'll gae you 500 smackeroonies.'

'Wow.' An expression of excitement appeared on Otis' pale face. 'You're on. When do ah start?'

'In five minutes. Get your gear on,' ordered Nellie. 'An' here's a note o' this fellow's address,' she said, as a sheet of paper emerged from a briefcase in her hand. 'Now, oan yer bike, Sherlock.'

✿ ✿ ✿

'Ah'm overwhelmed by the ridiculousness o' yer opinions!' Nellie ranted at James 'Ben' Nevis, the Convenor of Economy, Energy and Tourism, a man with a striking profile accentuated by a Tenerife tan and, by now, blinking bright blue eyes. 'We are not running a balloon factory ye know, though sometimes ah wonder. Ah think Scottish politics has generated more jokes than ony other activity barring sex and religion.'

'But, First Minister, all I am saying is…'

Nellie held her nose with one hand and mimed flushing a toilet with the other.

'Mister "Nevis" let me remind you we are here today to discuss ma manifesto.'

Nellie looked around the table in the meeting room. Her eyes narrowed to a squint. Everyone of any note was there but all were clearly unenthusiastic about today's subject.

'Pay attention, you lot. If you want tae increase your popularity ah suggest you get oan ma bandwagon an' give this your full consideration, rather than jist sitting lookin' oot the windows. The only person ah ever met who progressed while lookin' through a window wis a bus driver ah knew.'

'First Minister,' interrupted Duddy, 'you have got to admit that your agenda demands are radical and quixotic, and nothing more than populist. Furthermore, you are causing many MSPs grief as the general public seem to have got the opinion we are not supporting you, and as a result are giving us hell with cyberbullying on Twitter.'

A frown like a brewing storm took over Nellie's features.

'But surely you want to take some actions, Mister Duddy, that for once are popular with the punters, erm, voters, and not just continually tax them to death. We need to make their lives as comfortable as possible. Just in case you didn't realise it that's why we're here in the Parliament, folks,' she smiled grimly.

She looked around, anger still darkening her eyes.

'Right, first of all ah want to discuss ma policy of changin' the voting age. Now...'

The First Minister's mobile rang. For a moment she hesitated before opting to answer it.

'Mum, it's Otis.'

'Ah'm in an important meetin' at the moment, Son.'

'But ah've got news on this Hitler fellow.'

'Right. Make it quick.'

'He was in Glasgow for a few days and now he's disappeared to America.'

Nellie switched off her phone. 'Shit!'

'Most politicians would turn up fur the opening o' a crisp packet.'

BIG NELLIE NELLIS

CHAPTER NINE

Love and the Royals

'Och, that'll be quite handy jist nippin' o'er the road frae the Parliament Building or goin' frae here at St Andrew's House tae the Palace of Holyrood Hoose,' observed Nellie. 'Better than going up tae Balmoral or doon tae Buckingham Palace, eh? An' sure it was awfa nice o' them tae ask me?'

'Well, Nellie, you must remember that all First Ministers are eventually invited to meet the Royals, but it's still quite an honour,' explained Razzle as they sat in Nellie's office talking about the Royal invitation.

'Now listen Nellie, you'll probably need to brush up on your etiquette and learn what the protocol is on such occasions. All I can tell you off the top of my head is that the traditional way of greeting them is to address them as Royal Highness. Then, if you are a man, you give a neck bow, and women do a small curtsy.'

'So, what do ah call them? An' will they call me Nellie or First Minister?'

'You refer to them as sir or ma'am. They're very formal, so it will be First Minister as far as they're concerned,' explained her PA.

'Who's all going to be there, Razzle?'

'I think it will be Prince William, Catherine and their four children. The audience will probably last only 15 minutes.'

'Oh, good. Ah like them. They're a nice wee family. Maybe the weans will call me Auntie Nellie. See yon Prince George Alexander Louis, ah think he's cute. Mind you, wi' a name like that he needs tae be able to fight in the playground.'

'Now, you do appreciate, Nellie that you just can't walk across the road to the Palace of Holyroodhouse. It wouldn't be right. You need to make some sort of appropriate entrance, so it will be the ministerial car, regardless whether you come from the Parliament or St Andrew's House. Anyway, it could be raining.'

'Are you sure, Razzle? The papers will think ah'm like that "Two Jags" fella.'

'Now, Nellie, when did you ever worry about anything like that?'

'Well, right now ah'm more worried about this investigator fella who apparently is in the States. You just never know what these guys can dig up. Ah mean, we all did some wild stuff in our youth, didn't we? Ah bet you got up to a bit o' nonsense yersell, Razzle.'

'Probably, Nellie. But you sound awfully worried, it's not like you. All ah'm really worried about is the future.' Razzle then hesitated for a moment. 'You know, our future… yours and mine.'

'That's awfa nice o' you sayin' that. Glad somebody cares,' smiled Nellie.

'Listen, Nellie, ah've got to tell you, and this is probably not the time, but I do care. I've got…well, feelings for you,' Razzle blurted out, his hair flopping down over a crimson face.

Nellie turned and looked at him, suddenly conscious of his embarrassment. She took her time before replying.

'Razzle, you have been my counsellor an' best friend for a while now, and ah must admit that what you've just called feelings, ah have for you, too. But ah thought it was only me.' And she leaned over, buried her head in his shoulder, and they fell into an embrace. Then their eyes locked into each other, revealing the longing that had been hidden.

Nellie was the first to break the silence. 'Right, Razzle, nae more o' this lovey dovey stuff... for the minute, anyway. Now, what else is on the agenda for today?'

Razzle looked down at his latest gizmo, a superfast tablet, and announced. 'You're not going to believe this, Nellie, but your next appointment today is with Norman MacLeod, the Principal Officer from the US Consulate in Edinburgh.'

'Heavens above, Razzle. Why is he here? Is this something to do with that Hitler fella's investigations? Ma heart's gone all of a flutter with this new found romance stuff, an' now it's starting to beat even faster.'

'Naw, naw, Nellie. This is standard practice,' replied a bemused Razzle. 'It's just like your meeting with the Royals. It's merely a courtesy call – that is unless you shot somebody when you lived in the States?'

'Naw, ya daft clown, but ah would have thought this

Norman MacLeod would have something better to do,'
replied a still worried Nellie. 'Ah mean, ah would've
thought he would be busy handin' oot replacement
passports to all those American tourists who've lost theirs.'

'Relax, Nellie. It'll just be a chat and a coffee. I've
ordered the best coffee our catering group can provide.
It's already on the table. Got to keep the Americans on
our side, you know.'

MacLeod proved to be a tall, tanned, and apparently
charming man of middle-age.

'First Minister, I am so delighted to make your
acquaintance.' The handshake was firm. 'We should have
met some time ago but I was overseas for a while then up
north here in Scotland. Now, please call me Norman.'

'Pleased to meet you, too, Norman,' replied Nellie.
'And ah would be most happy for you to call me Nellie.
May ah introduce ma Personal Assistant, Razzle Dazzle,
sorry, Fraser MacLeod.'

'So happy to meet you, too, Fraser. Another
MacLeod, eh? Now the first thing I should tell you both
is that I am the son of a Scots couple. Mum and Dad
came from Skye and immigrated to the States in the '50s.
So you'll understand I was over the moon when I got the
posting to a country which we always considered to be
the family homeland.'

'Nice to see someone of our clan doing so well, Mister
MacLeod,' smiled Razzle.

'Please call me Norman, and am I correct in assuming
they call you Razzle Dazzle?'

'Aye, true. It's a name someone called me some time ago and it seems to have stuck,' Razzle confirmed. 'Now, would you like some coffee, sir... sorry, Norman?'

'Well, I am here today not just to drink what I will assume will be your excellent coffee, but to bring you cordial greetings on behalf of President Milton and the American Government. I am of course, as you will know, just one of many Americans who have links with this wonderful country.'

'And we truly love the interest Americans have in Scotland, Norman,' replied Nellie with a smile. 'You have many wonderful cities and great scenic sites in the States. It's a superb country. But we're delighted you Americans love our golf courses, whisky and castles.'

'You're right, Nellie,' agreed the Principal Officer. 'And I have to tell you that only last week I visited the ancient Dunvegan Castle on the Isle of Skye, which you may know, is the seat of the chief of the Clan MacLeod. MacLeods from all over the world visit there every four years for our Clan Parliament. So you see, Nellie, I'm a member of a sort of Scottish Parliament just like you.'

'Didn't know that,' replied Nellie. 'Very interesting. Ah've got to say that we have some of what ah would call numpties in our Parliament. What about yours?'

'Well, you will understand, Nellie – and Razzle here will certainly appreciate – that all our members are of a very high calibre. After all,' he laughed, 'they're all MacLeods. Isn't that right, Razzle?'

Razzle beamed and Nellie smiled. Here was a man

they both liked. Certainly one that they reckoned they
could do business with.

* * *

The Palace of Holyroodhouse is the Monarch's official
residence in Scotland. Like the Parliament Building
it stands at the end of the Royal Mile against the
spectacular backdrop of Arthur's Seat.

The State apartments are furnished with numerous
fine paintings and other works of art, and are used by
the Monarch and other members of the Royal Family for
official ceremonies and entertaining.

The Morning Drawing Room is where the Royals
give private audiences and it was here that Nellie,
First Minister of Scotland, met the Cambridges. She
remembered Razzle's instructions and curtsied to the
Duke, said good morning, ma'am to the Duchess,
beamed at the children, and immediately felt quite at
home. So much so that the Royals were somewhat taken
aback when Nellie informed the children that she was
their 'Auntie Nellie.'

'You must be George,' Auntie Nellie said to the
eldest, 'and of course you're Charlotte,' she observed,
looking down at the young princess. Then she turned her
attention to the twins, Charles and Alice. 'My, you two
are fairly growing up.'

'I didn't know we had an Aunt called Nellie,'
ventured George.

'Oh, yes, George. And ah come from Glasgow.'

'Were you once a little girl in Glasgow?' asked Charlotte.

William and Catherine smiled. This audience with Scotland's First Minister was certainly different from the usual dull affairs.

'Yes, dear,' Auntie Nellie continued. 'It was quite a while ago, mind you.'

'What was the name of your pony?' asked George.

Auntie Nellie was almost stumped for once but managed to recover. 'Well, ah didn't actually have a pony. You see my house was quite small so we just had a dog.'

'Was it a corgi?' queried Charlotte.

'No, dear. It was a breed called "mongrel".'

The Duke and the Duchess laughed, clearly enjoying this exchange with their children.

'Please be seated, First Minister,' said the Duke, 'and we'll sit, too. Now, can we offer you some refreshment?'

'That would be nice, sir,' replied Nellie politely, sitting down on an ornate red and gold chair. As if by magic an equerry appeared, taking orders from the Royals before asking Nellie what she would like.

'Ah'll have a double' Nellie hesitated. Mmmm, perhaps not, she thought. After all it was only just after 11.00am. Pity. 'Ah'll have a double latté, please.'

'Auntie Nellie.' A hand was tugging at her skirt. She looked and there was young Alice obviously keen to ask a question.

'Yes, dear,' replied Nellie, while at the same time

wondering if that was the correct way to address a young Royal.

'Auntie Nellie, what was the name of your dog?' Alice was obviously the more outgoing of the twins.

'Well, it was called "Scruff."'

'Why was it called Scruff, Auntie Nellie?' asked a persistent Alice now transfixed by the visitor.

Nellie thought a bit before answering.

'It was called Scruff because ma faither, sorry father, said that we were surrounded by scruff where we lived, and, if ah remember rightly, Scruff was a bit scruffy, too.'

'Come here, Alice,' came the voice of the Duchess. 'Don't pester our guest with questions.' Turning to Nellie she said. 'First Minister, you may not know this but I am a regular visitor to your Facebook profile. It's very interesting.'

'Thanks, ma'am,' replied Nellie. 'Actually my PA keeps it up to date for me.'

'I saw you were on *Desert Island Discs* so I made a point of listening to it. Loved your choice of music, especially "Nellie the Elephant." It's always been a favourite of mine, even as a child.'

'Was there really an elephant called the same as you, Auntie Nellie?' piped up Alice.

'It appears so, dear. And it ran away to join a circus.'

'Were you ever in a circus, Auntie Nellie?'

The First Minister almost responded by saying that she was in one at present. However she opted to reply politely, 'No dear.'

At this a footman appeared and stood just outside the now open door. Nellie got the hint. Her 15 minutes with the Royals was over.

Nellie shook hands with the Duke and Duchess and opted to give each of the children a hug before being shown out. Stuff this protocol business, she had reasoned; weans need a wee cuddle.

It was some days later that a drawing arrived in the mail at St Andrew's House. It was addressed 'For the personal attention of the First Minister'.

When Nellie opened the envelope, she found inside a child's drawing of an elephant beneath which was printed, 'To Anty Nelly, luv Alice Wales.'

'Isn't that sweet,' remarked Nellie, quite touched by the gesture.

'Aye,' observed Razzle. 'And if you're ever stuck for money in the future, Nellie, you could probably get a few bob for that on eBay.'

'Listen, Razzle, if ah'm ever stuck for money in the future, ah've now got you to fall back on. Eh!' And she winked while blowing him a kiss.

'Not all politicians are annoying...
some are dead.'

BIG NELLIE NELLIS

CHAPTER TEN

Intrigue

THROUGH HIS SLEEP he heard the ping of a text arriving. He ignored it and turned over.

It was not until the following morning at breakfast he opted to look at his phone, only to discover the text had come from MacSnape in the States. It read, 'Possible lead. Will keep you informed.'

Hope he's finally on to something, thought Duddy, before ruminating; could he not have been more specific? What a frustrating message. So he sent a text back... 'Please give details.' It was only as he was having a second coffee that he remembered there was a five hour difference. Their investigator would now be tucked up in bed.

Later, as he entered the Parliament Building, he saw the First Minister getting into her ministerial car along with Razzle Dazzle. Both were laughing. Bet these two have something going, he thought. If this sleuth really has dug up something interesting, they may not be smiling for much longer.

Normally in a meeting the Labour Leader would have his mobile switched off or set on silent mode, but the message from the private investigator had so intrigued him, giving him hope of a breakthrough, that when his phone buzzed during a discussion on Scotland's fishing industry, he immediately, somewhat rudely, produced it from his pocket. It was from MacSnape. 'Cannot give details. Possible national security situation.'

What in the world does that mean, he pondered? And for the remaining time of the meeting his thoughts were elsewhere, his fingers drumming on the table, and certainly not on North Sea fishing stocks and quotas.

When the meeting finished, he was out of the conference room like a shot, phone at his ear, arranging a meeting with Neil Forbes and the hack Henry Spiro to bring them up to date.

Meanwhile Nellie and Razzle had gone to Livingstone on a visit to a high-tech factory which manufactured energy efficient products. Business had expanded at the facility and Nellie was to open an extension to the main building which now housed another 200 newly hired workers. The press were out in force, and Nellie duly swapped banter with employees before posing for a 'team photograph' with all of the employees in what proved to be a blizzard of photo flashes.

Then it was time for coffee and a Danish with Raymond Ross the CEO, an impressive young man of around Otis age wearing a striped shirt, double-breasted suit, with a blue silk handkerchief in the top pocket. Never one to miss a trick Nellie enquired politely if there would be any future vacancies as she had a son who was looking for an executive position, preferable in the distribution side of the business? Unfortunately, she explained, he wasn't available at present as he was involved in a valuable research project. Raymond Ross promised he would most certainly look and see if his skills could be used in the company.

As they talked about the company's future in Scotland, and possible incentives that the CEO would prefer the Scottish Government to introduce, Nellie's mobile rang. She glanced at the screen. It was Otis.

'Excuse me,' she said to her host, getting to her feet and walking to a corner of the room. 'Yes, Otis, you always seem to call when ah'm in meetings. What is it now?'

'Hi, Mum.' Nellie could hardly hear him. He appeared to be whispering.

'Speak up, Son, you're very faint. And what is that noise ah can hear in the background?'

'I'm in a café in the New Town. I'm sitting next to those, well, 'you-know-who' guys.'

'Good. That's what ah'm paying you to do,' replied Nellie.

'They're sitting with another fellow who is busy typing on some high-tech bit of kit, and I heard him mention you a few times.'

Nellie could feel her hackles rising and she arched her well-plucked eyebrows. 'And just what does this other guy look like, Son?'

'Bit rough, with a scar running from his mouth across his chin, Mum.'

Nellie immediately got the picture. The third guy was probably that Spiro fellow who had asked a question at a press conference some time ago. A nasty bit of work if ever she saw one. Her brow creased in a frown of annoyance.

'Well done, Son. Tell you what, see if you possibly can take a photo of them together. Watch how you do it, ah don't want them to see you.'

'No bother, Mum. See you.' And the conversation finished.

Nellie apologised to the CEO for the interruption.

'Affairs of state,' she explained with a smile.

She was somewhat relieved when eventually the visit was over and she was seated once more in the ministerial car with Razzle. Quickly she explained the latest situation to her PA while searching her racing mind for the next move. This whole thing could be leading to a potential disaster.

❀ ❀ ❀

The café had acquired a reputation for excellent beverages and service in its upmarket setting.

Duddy, Forbes and Spiro sat huddled together, deliberating on the possible interpretation of Adolf's texts. It was proving an impossible task.

After much debate the three conspirators finally agreed that a further urgent text be sent to MacSnape. Without clarification of the situation they had no information to move on. The text which they agreed on read, 'What does security situation mean? Essential you provide specific details.' Then a frustrated Duddy added a further sarcastic sentence: 'Is this about terrorist activity in the States, *mein Führer*!!?'

Almost immediately a reply was received.

> Cannot comment at present. Back in two days with all the info you will ever need. Expect major bonus!

'Sounds as though he's hit the jackpot, eh?' smiled a jubilant Neil Forbes, a note of excitement in his voice.

'Let's wait and see,' cautioned an exasperated Duddy pausing to let the wording of the text sink in. 'Don't want to count our chickens just yet, do we?' Then he suddenly looked up and commented. 'Hey! Did that young guy at the next table just take a photo of us?' They all looked in time to see the back of a man in motorcycle leathers slipping out the door.

'Don't be silly, Duddy,' replied Neil. 'Your nerves are getting to you on this thing.' Turning to Henry Spiro he said, 'Listen, Henry, what Duddy and I will do is have a debriefing session with our man once he returns. Get it all from the horse's mouth so to speak. But the thing you must understand is we are already significantly out of pocket employing this private investigator. It is proving much more expensive than we thought it would be. Can't charge everything through our expense accounts. So we would need a contribution from you. Then we can give you all the info you need.'

'How much?' scowled Spiro.

Without any consultation with Neil Forbes, Duddy said, 'Ten grand.'

'Wow,' said Spiro, 'it would need to be some story for that! Remember, gents, that you really need me to publicise the tit bits.'

'True. Though we could no doubt use other journalists. If it's really juicy the press would bite our hands off to get a big scoop.'

'Sure,' replied the sleazy hack, grinning. 'But you must also remember, gents, I know who the two eminent politicians are who hired the private detective in the first place.'

'That sounds a bit like blackmail, Spiro,' growled Duddy.

'Put it any way you wish, the truth is we all need each other on this one.'

'Okay, we take your point,' said a resigned Duddy. 'However, are you prepared to come up with hard cash?'

'Of course,' smiled Spiro with little hesitation. 'I'll put up five grand with another five thrown in if it proves sensational.'

The two politicians sat searching each other's eyes intently before giving a grudging nod to the deal.

'Right, we'll be in touch once we find out what MacSnape is on about,' concluded Forbes.

'Fine, guys. Then I'll be on my way. Just let me know where and when and I'll be there with the money,' said the journalist with a grin which only further highlighted the scar around his mouth. Then he rose abruptly, and left the café with the two worried politicians watching his departure.

Neil Forbes was the first to speak.

'It looks as though we may finally have something on Nellis, but I must confess, Duddy, there's something in my water that's worrying me.'

'If MSPs would only talk when they think, the Scottish Parliament would be a nice quiet place.'

BIG NELLIE NELLIS

CHAPTER ELEVEN

Exposed

'HELLO, DUDDY SPEAKING.'

'Hello there.'

'Yes, hello there, who is speaking, please?

'It's ehm, me.'

'And just who is me?

'Neil Forbes of course. Didn't we have a similar phone conversation some time ago?'

'Sorry, Neil, didn't recognise your voice. Glad you phoned. I must confess I'm getting concerned. Haven't heard a dickie-bird from our friend in America. I thought we would have all his data by now.'

'That is a worry. I've had Spiro on the phone twice asking if we've any details yet,' replied Neil Forbes, his voice showing some strain.

'Well, I've sent MacSnape two texts, a couple of emails and tried phoning him,' moaned the Labour Leader. 'Nothing so far. I think his phone is switched off.'

'My worry,' continued Neil, 'is that he has got on to something really big and is negotiating some deal with a publishing house.'

'True,' replied Duddy. 'But at least if that was the case and there is any sort of scandal, that would get it out into the media. Remember, the object of the exercise is hopefully to bring down "you-know-who."'

'Of course,' said Forbes, 'but let's give it another two days and if there is still nothing then we should meet again and discuss our options. However, let's be a bit more optimistic. Our phones could ring at any moment, Duddy, and it could be our man on the line with some interesting details.'

'Aye, well, let's hope so.'

❀   ❀   ❀

The American Consulate in Scotland was established in Edinburgh in 1798. It is located on Regent Terrace, by Calton Hill, quite near to St Andrew's House.

The invitation to a meeting with the Consulate Principal Officer had been most unexpected, especially as he had only recently paid a courtesy call on the First Minister. As it was a beautiful sunny day in the capital, Nellie opted to walk the short distance to Regent Terrace, without Razzle, but closely followed by her security officer.

Once at the Consulate, the First Minister was received most courteously before being shown into the Principal Officer's large, wood-panelled, ornate study. Looking around, Nellie couldn't help but notice that on the wall, behind Norman MacLeod's desk, hung a large portrait of the current President of America.

'First Minister, thank you so much for accepting my invitation,' said the Principal Officer coming forward and shaking Nellie's hand. The grip was firm enough but she felt the atmosphere surprisingly formal.

'Please be seated. Would you care for a refreshment?'

'That would be good, Norman. A glass of Glenmorangie would be appreciated,' Nellie smiled. 'It was actually a pleasure to get out of the office on such a nice day and get a breath of fresh air. Ah'm happy you invited me.'

'Quite so,' said the now serious Principal Officer. 'Let me get your drink before we start,' and he went to a drinks cabinet and poured out two large whiskies. 'Now, First Minister, you are obviously wondering why I requested this meeting, so I will get straight to the point because I know you are a busy lady. The Consulate has been contacted by the CIA regarding an individual they have recently arrested.'

Nellie sat back in her chair. Here it all comes, she said to herself.

'Well, First Minister, apparently this person was in possession of sensitive personal information relative to a senior politician in the States.'

The Principal Officer looked keenly at Nellie. Her demeanour hadn't changed.

'First Minister, I have got to tell you that somehow you were mentioned in the documents recovered by the CIA.'

'Now that is truly amazing,' said Nellie coolly. 'Why would that be?'

'First Minister, you are the most senior politician in Scotland and this is somewhat embarrassing for me. However, I understand you have one child, is that correct?'

Nellie nodded slowly. Play this coolly, she rationalised.

'Let me come to the point, First Minister. It is alleged that this child, a boy I believe, could be the offspring of this senior politician.'

Nellie said nothing.

'Of course, First Minister, this could all be a silly misunderstanding but I wonder if I could have your further co-operation on this matter... just to clear it all up, you understand.'

'Principal Officer,' said Nellie, adopting a similar formal approach, 'you will need to tell me how this person who has been arrested apparently came by this information.'

The American leaned forward on his desk and clasped her hand.

'Nellie, if I may once again call you that, you must understand that although I am a diplomat this is not easy for me. The confidential information I have received is that a couple of your political opponents here in Scotland hired this fellow, a private investigator from Edinburgh I believe, to find out about your early life in the States. He apparently tracked down your best friend from school to whom you allegedly confided that the child you were bearing at that time was a result of a liaison with this particular politician.'

He stopped and looked again at Nellie. She leaned back and swivelled her chair, calmly mulling the situation over as she sipped her whisky. Where was all this going to lead, she pondered?

'Cards on the table, Nellie. The CIA would like a blood and DNA sample from your son. Personally I will understand if you say no, and that your private life is being invaded. Now we most certainly don't want any diplomatic incidents with our oldest ally. You know, the "special arrangement" our countries have and all that.'

The diplomat sat back awaiting a response from Nellie. She made up her mind. It was all going to come out in the wash, anyway, so... what the hell! Heavens, what would Otis say when asked to provide samples? That would really get him going.

'Okay, Norman, ah agree. Let's clear this all up. Ah'll talk tae my son, see if he'll agree.'

❊ ❊ ❊

It was much later that evening when Otis arrived back at Bute House. Nellie heard his motorbike outside, then the footsteps on the stairs.

'Right, Otis, where have you been?' she immediately demanded.

'Listen, Mum, for heaven's sake I'm a big boy now. Got to let off a bit of steam, you know. Anyway, there has been nothing happening regarding these guys. The 'Hitler' fellow is nowhere to be seen and the others have not met up since that time I told you about in the café.'

'Okay, Son. Fine, cool it. Ah want you to sit down fur a minute.'

'But Mum, I'm tired. Want to get to my bed,' moaned Otis.

'This is important, Son, very important. Sit doon an' listen to me.'

'This had better be good,' he moaned. Then looking at his mother's serious face Otis did as instructed and sat.

'Otis, for most of your life you have moaned that you don't know who your faither is.'

'Don't tell me he's turned up, Mum?' Otis asked his face lightening.

'No, Son. But we may be able to – shall we say – help track him down. That is if you are prepared tae assist?'

'But how can I help, Mum?' asked a perplexed Otis.

'Well, it's relatively simple. As you know ah became pregnant while ah wis in the States. So, ah wis talkin' to the American Consulate guy today, and if you go to the Consulate in Regent Terrace they will take a blood and DNA sample from you. Then they will hopefully be able to identify your faither from the large DNA banks that they apparently have in the US,' Nellie said, with her fingers crossed.

Otis looked directly at his mother. 'Mum, you're making me nervous. I'm not too sure after all if I really want to know who he is now I think on it. Could be anybody.'

'Otis. Ah like men, but don't you dare imply ah wis promiscuous!' Nellie said sharply.

'Sorry, Mum. Okay, I'll do it. When should I go?'

'Tomorrow, Son. They're expecting you. Just ask for Norman MacLeod the Principal Officer. Ah'll phone him and let him know you'll pop in. And by the way, print out a copy of the photo you took of the guys in the café and give it to Mister MacLeod, would you?'

'Sure, though I don't understand why he might need that photo? Now I am never going to get to sleep tonight, Mum, thinking about all of this. Actually it's quite exciting.'

❀ ❀ ❀

Air Force One, a Boeing 747–200B, landed at Maryland's Andrews Air Force Base shortly after 2.00pm, Eastern Standard Time.

Nellie and Otis quickly disembarked from the super exclusive presidential jet, more like a luxurious hotel than a plane with its phenomenal facilities including a gym, conference rooms and even a doctor and nurse on board. Both Nellie and Otis took some time to profusely thank the crew and staff for their attention and superb hospitality. The food had been mouth-watering. Razzle had made Nellie promise that she would only have one wee whisky on the flight. In the end she had behaved herself up to a point but had two.

Security was tight as they then climbed the steps into the confines of 'Marine One', the presidential helicopter that would take them to the White House. Everything had gone so quickly in the last few days but finally they were approaching journey's end.

'Marine One' landed smoothly onto the lawn of the White house and mother and son were immediately security checked.

'Ah didnae even bring a haggis,' Nellie informed the unsmiling security officer.

A presidential aide appeared and took them along a series of corridors into the Oval Office in the West Wing. Both Scots were immediately disappointed at their first impression of this relatively small room, with its three south-facing windows behind the President's desk and a fireplace at the north end. Maybe the Scottish Parliament Building isn't so bad after all, thought Nellie.

'If you would kindly be seated,' requested the aide, a pleasant, young, extremely well dressed black man, 'I will get you coffees and then inform President Milton and his wife that you have arrived. I know that they are both immensely looking forward to meeting you.'

A few minutes later, as Nellie and Otis sat quietly sipping their coffees while still taking in their surroundings, the west door of the Oval office opened and in came President George Milton and his wife, Ruth, a tall attractive blonde. Nellie guessed she would be around her own age.

As Nellie and Otis stood, the President and his wife halted in their tracks, both looking intently at Otis. Nellie looked from the President to her son. Just like peas in a pod, as she had always suspected. There was no doubt that here was Milton's offspring, a younger version of the American himself.

George Milton's face crumbled and tears streamed down his cheeks as he stepped forward and embraced Otis. Similarly Otis was clearly overcome by the occasion. At long last he had found his father, and what a father at that! It was some time before the most powerful man in the world could compose himself properly to shake Nellie's hand and introduce his wife.

'I am so, so, delighted to meet you, Otis, or should I say, my son, and of course First Minister Nellis. You know, Ruth here is the love of my life but, unfortunately, we have never been blessed with children. Since learning of Otis' existence, Ruth and I have discussed this new situation in detail, and I'm pleased to tell you she is also thrilled that we now have a son.' At that the President's wife stepped forward to smile and give her new stepson a warm hug. Then George Milton turned to Nellie.

'Isn't it amazing how things turn out,' he said. 'What I mean is that hopefully we all can share the love of Otis.' And he looked at Nellie for approval.

'Well, Mister President, obviously Otis will need to get to know this part of his family better, but I can tell you that he certainly shares his love among plenty of, eh, other people in Edinburgh. So, ah have a feeling this is going to work out well all round.'

'I believe it will, First Minister Nellis. Oh, sorry, excuse me for a minute,' said the President as he vigorously blew his nose. 'You see I have terrible allergies.'

Nellie glanced at Otis – and smiled.

❊　❊　❊

'We have waited for over a week now and heard nothing further from America, so I thought it best we review the situation,' Duddy informed Neil Forbes and Henry Spiro as they sat in the comfortable lounge of Duddy's Edinburgh flat. The two politicians had opted to invite the journalist as absolutely nothing was happening, and he might have a bright idea or two.

All were clearly frustrated, for by this time they had envisaged they would have been informed of some sort of story with real meat in it, one they and the press could get their teeth into. But there was nothing further. Unfortunately, they were still limited to pouring over the wording of the out-of-date texts received, trying once again to interpret what the contents could possibly mean. It was proving really difficult if not impossible to think of a further move at this stage.

'So, what can we now possibly do? Got any bright ideas, Henry? You see Duddy and I can't possible leave Parliament and suddenly go hunting around in the States, but perhaps you could. Or, do we just keep sending messages that never get answers, eh?'

But the answer arrived at that very moment. The outside door of the apartment suddenly shook. They all looked up as they heard it shake again. This time they heard the hinges flying off, just before the lounge door burst open revealing two wardrobe-like individuals whose expensive suits did little to hide bulging biceps and holsters.

'CIA,' said the two men producing identity wallets. 'On your feet. Names, and make it fast.' The voice was American, the attitude threatening.

'Now look here, you can't just break…' began a shaken Neil Forbes.

'Shut up! Your names, quick,' growled the larger of the two gorillas – clearly the boss.

'Our names are Duddy, Forbes and this is a journalist friend, Henry Spiro,' spluttered out Neil Forbes.

The bossman jabbed a finger at a slip of paper. Then he produced a photograph and consulted with his partner.

'Yip, these are the targets.'

Duddy caught a glimpse of the photo. It showed the three of them in the café in the New Town.

'We are CIA agents. You have been identified as suspects trying to undermine the American government.'

'Don't be ridiculous,' protested a white-faced Duddy. 'We don't know what you are talking about.'

'Listen, pal. Do you know a prisoner by the name of MacSnape?'

'A prisoner? For heaven's sake, what's he been accused of?'

'So, you obviously know him. He's in the same boat as you. Communicating with other suspected persons and making threats to our national security stateside. Don't you guys realise our people monitor electronic communications? Right, turn around till we get the cuffs on. We have a vehicle waiting outside.'

'You can't do this,' further protested Duddy his hands trembling. 'Spiro is a respectable journalist and we are democratically elected Scottish politicians. Furthermore, we are on UK soil. This is not America.'

'Just in case you are in any doubt, pilgrims, this operation has been personally approved by the President of the United States and your very own First Minister. You guys are in it right up to your necks.'

❀ ❀ ❀

'So, Otis is staying on at the White House with the Miltons, Nellie?'

'Aye, and he's as happy as Larry. Going round the social scene in Washington accompanied by bodyguards. Now his faither can worry about him for a change.'

'Nellie, maybe you could fill me in on the background to all of this? I'm still confused,' said Razzle as they sat in Nellie's office going over the day's dairy.

'Okay, ah'll tell you how it all happened, Razzle. It's only right you know if we are going to have a future together. You see, ah wis at this Democratic Party convention in a Howard Johnston Hotel in New York. Now, ah must admit ah had quite a bit to drink in the bar beforehand. The candidate standing for the Senate wis this southerner, George Milton. Charisma coming oot of his ears. Would charm the birds oot of the trees. Had everybody in the palm o' his hand. Well, the rally wis held in the ballroom on the sixth floor an', efter it finished, ah chatted to a few friends before going over to the elevator, you know, the lift, to go doon to the foyer. Well, ah wis in the elevator on ma own, had just pressed the button, when at the last minute as the doors were closing, in comes this George Milton looking like a million dollars. So there wis me, a few drinks in me and star struck with this guy. He came up, put his arm around me an' before ah knew it, well, the bugger had pressed the stop button, an' there was the two of us going at it. Afterwards, the one thing ah remembered wis the name on the elevator control panel: "Otis." So, there you have it, Razzle.'

'The reason MSPS find it difficult to think is that they haven't had any previous experience.'

BIG NELLIE NELLIS

CHAPTER TWELVE

Hold the front page

IT DIDN'T SOUND like much of a scandal at the start, more an intriguing mystery.

The initial reports were obviously litigation-conscious which held back some of the juicy detail. When the situation was finally clarified, it roared through the world media at maximum warp. The press just loved it. Everyone loved it, apart from Nellie herself.

All news programmes, regional, national and world-wide, led with the story.

The media gleefully jumped on the situation, digging up other stories of the past about famous figures having affairs. Every day more soundbites arrived. In fact it became open season on many MSPs private lives, terrifying the shit out of the rest o' them. As a result, many smoke-and-mirrors merchants finally had their secret lives exposed.

The 'Sundays' produced exclusive colour magazines detailing the life of President George Milton from womb to the present. Somehow, various photos of Nellie's early life also appeared.

Many things were happening, including Raymond Ross ringing Nellie's office to ask if Otis was still looking for a senior position? The company would now be delighted to have the son of the American president as their chairman! Fat chance now, thought Nellie.

Duddy and Forbes had been released from custody but immediately resigned from the Government and left politics in disgrace.

Henry Spiro was rumoured to be abroad, writing a book.

The increase in American tourists visiting Scotland was another aspect of the 'Otis Effect', as one newspaper headline had put it. Exports in whisky and Irn-Bru significantly increased, and there was even talk of the States raising its ban on the importation of haggis.

Then after some months public morality raised its head, and suddenly Nellie's enemies had a feeling of *schadenfreude*. The country was split between to enjoying the startling news and wishing Nellie well, and some of the population who were starting to feel uneasy about the whole thing.

Nellie, with her never-ending ability to judge the public mood, knew it would soon be time to bid farewell. But, she determined, not before she managed to drive through some more of her policies. And it was to this end that she had Razzle arrange another meeting with the senior politicians remaining in the Scottish Government.

On the day the meeting room in the Parliament was full to the gunnels. Word had got out that a significant announcement would be made by the First Minister. Even the press had got hold of the speculation. As Nellie got to her feet, a sea of expectant faces looked up at the First Minister. She looked around,with everyone all ears.

'Ladies and gentlemen, first of all thank you for coming to this extraordinary meeting. Today I have two significant announcements to make. Both personal.

'The first one is this,' and Nellie raised her left hand to display a sparkling engagement ring. This caused a storm of applause and some shouts of 'who's the unlucky man, then?' and a further comment of, 'is George getting divorced?' was heard.

'Aye,' continued Nellie, 'Razzle and masell are engaged to be married. An' don't ask if ah'll be a white bride,' she laughed.

'As usual ah'm gonnae give you all hell before ah tell you the next item. Got to keep you lot on your toes, you know. By this time you probably expect nothing less.' Nellie paused for effect.

'Ah believe this Parliament has improved but is still in the intellectual doldrums. Huffing, plotting and hissy fits still go on amongst some clique-forming politicians. Many are delusional, hence the place still has a few megalomaniacs, egotists, backstabbers and wannabe despots, but after all, as ah've come to realise, that is just politics for you worldwide. Also, sometimes Parliament does lose its moral compass, but as you now know, ah'm perhaps not in a position to lecture you on that.

'But let me be positive and say ah have discovered in my time here that there are also many good forward-thinking politicians amongst you; many of them in this room today. People who are genuinely here for the benefit of their constituents and Scotland.

'They say that it's not all over till the fat lady sings. Just a few points on that wan. Ah'm no' fat, just well built, and ah cannae sing. An' ah have not quite finished ma performance here at the Parliament.

'This takes me to my second point today, and that is, it is almost time for me to step aside.' An excited murmur ran round the room. The First Minister continued.

'During the last few months there has been plenty of publicity about my relationship some years ago with the present American president. This episode has cost two of Scotland's most prominent politicians their careers. In fact they are lucky not to be languishing in prison if you ask me. Whit a pair o' humdingers!

'However, this Parliament needs to get on with the very important task of governing our lovely land. My remaining as First Minister is clearly proving a distraction, an' ah suspect a few people will probably be happy to see the back o' me. So, here's the deal, boys and girls. Ah came into this Parliament with what ah called ma "shopping list", in reality ma manifesto. So far ah have had very little of it passed, and for some items ah have red lines under them. As far as ah'm concerned they are the core manifesto commitments of ma AGSTLO Party. So, ah want you all to tell me how many of them you are prepared to vote for in the short term. If ah think what you offer is okay then the prize is ma resignation. What a bargain, eh?

'Over the next week ah want you to put your heads thegither and tell me what you will accept. Just so there is no misunderstanding, you should clearly know that if it's "no-go", then it's "no-go" with me, too. Okay?

'So, now it's over to you.' Nellie chose not to sit down but abruptly left the room. Afterwards some MSPs would swear she had tears in her eyes.

The offer proved too good to ignore for MSPs. A number of cross party meetings were hastily arranged with various options being put forward, ranging from non-acceptance of any further of Nellie's manifesto proposals to accepting as many as six of them. Finally, after great deliberation and negotiation, it was decided that extra money would be provided to councils to ensure all identified pot holes would be filled in by the following day, the Government would also provide funding for free transport on Scotland's ferries, buses and trains for everyone over 60 who wasn't working, and an invitation would be sent to Sir Andy Murray to become Scotland's Sports Minister.

Nellie duly accepted their conclusions and gracefully stepped down from her position as First Minister and resigned as a MSP.

And so, relative peace reigned once more at the Scottish Parliament.

'MSPS are all tooled up. Aye, they use weapons of mass distraction!'

BIG NELLIE NELLIS

BBC News Bulletin

'We interrupt this programme to inform you that Jacques Beauton, President of the European Commission, has died suddenly of an apparent heart attack. President Beauton collapsed during an exchange with a journalist at a press conference in the Hague, when Mister Beauton was informed that the former First Minister of Scotland, Mrs Nellie MacLeod, is standing to become a MEP.'

'MSPS always stand for what they think the voters will fall for.'

BIG NELLIE NELLIS

CHAPTER THIRTEEN

How the Scottish Parliament actually operates

THE SCOTTISH PARLIAMENT comprises 129 elected representatives at the Parliament Building in Holyrood.

It is set at the foot of Edinburgh's famous Royal Mile in front of the spectacular Holyrood Park and Salisbury Crags. Constructed from a mixture of steel, oak and granite, this complex and controversial building was, when opened, hailed as one of the most innovative designs in the UK.

Drawing inspiration from the surrounding landscape, the flower paintings by Charles Rennie Macintosh and the upturned boats on the seashore, Enric Miralles, one of the world's leading architects, developed a design that he said was 'a building growing out of the land'.

The Debating Chamber is where meetings of the full Parliament are held and MSPs can debate topical issues and decide on new laws. The chamber is located directly above the Main Hall. It is purpose built to meet the needs of the Parliament, the public and the media. The debating chamber contains 131 seats and desks, arranged in a hemicycle layout for MSPs, with two seats for the Lord Advocate and the Solicitor General who are unelected and therefore cannot vote. There are also four broadcasting booths.

The First Minister, Scottish Cabinet Members and Law Officers sit in the front row in the middle section of the chamber. The largest party in the Parliament sits in the middle of the semicircle, with opposing parties on either side. The Presiding Officer, parliamentary clerks and officials sit opposite members at the front of the debating chamber.

On the upper level of the Debating Chamber there is a gallery with seating for 225 members of the public, 18 invited guests and 34 members of the media.

Parliament typically sits on Tuesdays, Wednesdays and Thursdays from early January to late June and from early September to mid-December, with two-week recesses in April and October.

The unique façade of the MSPs office accommodation has become the iconic image of Holyrood. Here there are 114 projecting bay windows. MSPs occupy 108 of the offices and the others are used as party resource rooms. Each bay office has a window seat and shelving. This area was designed as a 'contemplation space' by the architect, Enric Miralles.

The Parliament is the law-making body in Scotland for devolved matters, and scrutinises the work of the Scottish Government which is formed from the party holding most seats. The Government is normally led by a First Minister who chooses Cabinet Secretaries and Ministers.

St Andrew's House, located on the southern flank of
Calton Hill in Regent Road, is on the east side of Princes
Street overlooking Holyrood Park and accommodates
part of the Scottish Government. This includes the office
of the First Minister of Scotland and Deputy Minister of
Scotland along with the private offices of all the Cabinet
Secretaries. The building now accommodates some
1,400 civil servants. St Andrew's House stands on the
site of the former Calton Jail.

Scottish Parliament elections are normally held every
four years with every voter in Scotland being allowed
two votes on an AMS (Additional Member System) basis.
One vote is for their constituency MSP, the other for the
Region. Every voter in Scotland is represented by one
constituency MSP and seven regional MSPs. Constituents
may contact any of the eight MSPs who represent them.

Of the 129 MSPs, 73 are constituency MSPs and 56
represent the eight larger regional areas of the country.
Regional MSPs are chosen based on the number of votes
each party receives in each region.

After each election to the Scottish Parliament,
Parliament elects one MSP to serve as 'Presiding Officer'
(the equivalent of the 'Speaker' at Westminster) and two
MSPs to act as deputies. All three are elected by a secret
ballot of the 129 MSPs. Principally the role of the
Presiding Officer is to chair the chamber proceedings.
This individual is also responsible for representing the
Parliament externally. When chairing meetings of the
Parliament and during debates, the Presiding Officer and

his/her deputies must be politically impartial. They are assisted by parliamentary clerks who give advice on how to interpret the standing orders that govern the proceedings of the meeting. A vote clerk sits in front of the Presiding Officer and operates the electronic voting equipment and chamber clocks.

Much of the work of the Scottish Parliament is done in committee. The role of the committees is to partly compensate for the lack of a second revising chamber. Their principal role is to take evidence from witnesses, conduct inquiries and scrutinise legislation.

The highlight of the week is *First Minister's Questions*, when MSPs have the opportunity to quiz/ probe/cross-examine the First Minister on any issue. Opposition leaders normally ask a general question of the First Minister to start off the proceedings followed by supplementary questions. Such a practice enables a 'lead-in' to the questioner, who then uses their supplementary question to ask the First Minister on any issue. The four initial general questions available to opposition leaders are:

- To ask the First Minister what engagements he/she has planned for the rest of the day.

- To ask the First Minister when he/she next plans to meet the Prime Minister of the United Kingdom and what issues they intend to discuss.

- To ask the First Minister when he/she next plans to meet the Secretary of State for Scotland and what issues they intend to discuss.
- To ask the First Minister what issues he/she intends to discuss at the next meeting of the Scottish Government Cabinet.

Following a referendum in 1997 in which the Scottish electorate gave their consent, a Scottish Parliament and devolved Scottish Government were established. This process of devolution was initiated to give Scotland a measure of self-governance in its domestic affairs resulting in the establishment of a post of First Minister to be the head of the devolved Scottish Government.

The First Minister of Scotland is the political leader and head of the Scottish Government. The First Minister chairs the Scottish Cabinet and is primarily responsible for the formation, development and presentation of Scottish Government policy.

The First Minister is nominated by the Scottish Parliament from among its members at the beginning of each term by means of an exhaustive ballot. In theory, any member of the Scottish Parliament can be nominated for First Minister. However, the Government must be answerable to, and acceptable to, the Scottish Parliament in order to gain access to exchequer funds. In practice the First Minister holds office as long as he or she retains the confidence of the chamber.

After the election of the Scottish Parliament, a First Minister must be nominated within a period of 28 days. Under the terms of the Scotland Act, if the Parliament fails to nominate a First Minister within this time frame, it will be dissolved and a fresh election held.

Further Big Nellie 'Whollyrude' observations

'The reason MSPS want re-elected is that they would hate to try and make a living under the bills they have passed.'

'What do you call a Glasgow underground train full of MSPS? Tubes who think they're Smarties!'

'A week in politics is a long time. But the weak in politics are along all the time!'

'Whit ah always say is, let sleeping MSPS lie!'

BIG NELLIE
HAS LEFT THE
BUILDING

Some other books published by **LUATH** PRESS

Last Tram tae Auchenshuggle!

Allan Morrison

Illustrated by Mitch Miller

ISBN 978-1-908373-04-5 PBK £7.99

Wur full! Everybuddy haud ontae a strap or yer man!

It's the end of the line for Glasgow's famous clippie, Big Aggie MacDonald, as her beloved trams are destined for the big depot in the sky.

Last Tram tae Auchenshuggle! is a trip down memory lane to 1962, with the Glasgow tram service about to come to an end. But Aggie wants to enjoy the last months on her beloved caurs, dishing out advice and patter with her razor-sharp wit to the unwary: the outspoken clippie who was never outspoken!

Big Aggie's tram is pure theatre, and the clippie is something else when it comes to dealing with fare dodgers, drunks, wee nyaffs, cheeky weans and highfalutin' wummen.

Get aff! O-f-f, aff! Dae ye no' undertaun' the Queen's English?

The historical realities of the Glasgow tramline are brought to life with Allan Morrison's hilarious patter. The last regular tram ran on 1 September 1962, and for the following three days a special service operated between Auchenshuggle and Anderston Cross. But even today the magic of the Glasgow trams has not been forgotten.

Haud ma Chips, Ah've Drapped the Wean! Glesca Grannies' Sayings, Patter and Advice

Allan Morrison

Illustrated by Bob Dewar

ISBN 978-1-908373-47-2 PBK £7.99

In yer face, cheeky, kindly, gallus, astute; that's a Glesca granny for you. Glesca grannies' communication is direct, warm, expressive, rich and often hilarious.

'Dinnae cross yer eyes. Ye'll end up like that squinty bridge.'

'Oor doctor couldnae cure a plouk oan a coo's erse.'

'This is me since yesterday.'

'That wan wid breastfeed her weans through the school railings.'

'Yer hair looks like straw hingin' oot a midden.'

'Ah'm jist twinty-wan an' ah wis born in nineteen-canteen.'

'The secret o' life is an aspirin a day, a wee dram, an' nae sex oan Sundays.'

Glesca grannies shoot from the mouth and get right to the point with their sayings, patter and advice. This book is your guide to the infallible wisdom of the Glesca granny.

Should've Gone Tae Specsavers, Ref!

Allan Morrison

Illustrated by Bob Dewar

ISBN 978-1-908373-73-1 PBK £7.99

The referee. You can't have a game without one. The most hated man (or woman) in football but you have to invite one to every game.

Enjoy a laugh at the antics and wicked humour of Scottish referee Big Erchie, a powerhouse at five foot five, and a top grade referee who strikes fear into the hearts of managers and players alike as he stringently applies the laws of the game.

But Big Erchie is burdened with a terrible secret… He's a Partick Thistle supporter.

'Goanae No Dae That!': The best of the best of those cracking Scottish sayings!

Allan Morrison

ISBN: 978-1-910021-57-6 PBK £7.99

The Scots have a unique way of communicating their feelings. Their sayings are cheeky, to the point, rude and always funny. Scotland's bestselling humour author is back with his latest collection of hilarious Scottish sayings.

'Away an' bile yer heid an' mak silly soup!'

'If you don't behave ah'll pawn ye an' sell the ticket.'

'That wan's in everything but the Co-operative windae!'

'If ah had your money ah wid burn ma ain.'

'Ye've goat a heid oan ye like a stair-heid.'

'The gemme's a bogie.'

'Yer cruisin' fur a bruisin'.'

'Ah'm that hungry ah could eat a scabbie-heided horse.'

'Castor oil cures everythin' but a widden leg.'

'Wan minute yer a peacock an' the next yer a feather duster.'

'Yer talkin' mince withoot a tattie in sight.'

'Lang may yer lum reek, an' may a wee moose never leave yer kitchen press wi' a tear in its ee.'

'Yer herr's mingin', hingin' an' clingin'.'

The Dean's Diaries: Being a True & Factual Account of the Doings & Dealings of the Dean & Dons of St Andrew's College, Edinburgh

Prof. David Purdie
Illustrated by Bob Dewar
ISBN: 978-1-910745-20-5 PBK £8.99

Meet the long-suffering Dean of St Andrew's College – an Edinburgh-based academic institution bursting with eccentricity, interdepartmental feuding and explosive disasters. The cantankerous Dean's rants and questionably reliable anecdotes provide an exceptionally witty account of academia in Edinburgh, effortlessly combining the realities of life in Scotland's capital city with the decidedly fantastical goings on at St Andrew's.

the general population of Scotland remains rightly proud of St Andrew's College, seeing in its fierce political incorrectness and general eccentricity a shield against the creeping gloom of the endarkenment.

RT HON. LORD FANSHAWE FRS

Follow the Dean and a raucous cast of staff and students through formal dinners, an attack from a giant squid, an antimatter accident, several cases of mistaken identity and countless further adventures in *The Dean's Diaries*.

If History was Scottish

Norma Ferguson
Illustrated by Bob Dewar
ISBN: 978-1-908373-67-0 PBK £7.99

Scots have made a huge contribution to the world – you only have to look at a tea towel listing the famous sons and daughters of the saltire to see that.

However, surprisingly, there is much that has taken place without its influence. This books seeks to show what could have happened if history was Scottish.

The famous figures and major events that have made an impact throughout the history of the world are seen through a uniquely comedic Caledonian perspective. The whole clanjamfrie of attributes associated with being Scottish – pawky, canny, contrary, gallus, aggressive, idealistic and maudlin – are used to revisit the battles, assassinations, explorations and inventions across the continents and centuries.

Some of those appearing are: JFK, MLK, Marie Antoinette, Neil Armstrong, Jesus, Lenin, The Beatles, Attila the Hun, Julius Caesar, Scott of the Antarctic, Rasputin, Albert Einstein, Queen Victoria, Hitler and Typhoid Mary.

Welcome to an alternative world, where all history is Scottish.

Luath Press Limited
committed to publishing well written books worth reading

LUATH PRESS takes its name from Robert Burns, whose little collie Luath (*Gael.*, swift or nimble) tripped up Jean Armour at a wedding and gave him the chance to speak to the woman who was to be his wife and the abiding love of his life. Burns called one of 'The Twa Dogs' Luath after Cuchullin's hunting dog in Ossian's *Fingal*. Luath Press was established in 1981 in the heart of Burns country, and now resides a few steps up the road from Burns' first lodgings on Edinburgh's Royal Mile. Luath offers you distinctive writing with a hint of unexpected pleasures.

Most bookshops in the UK, the US, Canada, Australia, New Zealand and parts of Europe either carry our books in stock or can order them for you. To order direct from us, please send a £sterling cheque, postal order, international money order or your credit card details (number, address of cardholder and expiry date) to us at the address below. Please add post and packing as follows: UK – £1.00 per delivery address; overseas surface mail – £2.50 per delivery address; overseas airmail – £3.50 for the first book to each delivery address, plus £1.00 for each additional book by airmail to the same address. If your order is a gift, we will happily enclose your card or message at no extra charge.

Luath Press Limited
543/2 Castlehill
The Royal Mile
Edinburgh EH1 2ND
Scotland
Telephone: 0131 225 4326 (24 hours)
email: sales@luath.co.uk
Website: www.luath.co.uk